Illicit Coterie

Elizabeth Renwick

Coterie Publishing LLC * USA

Grateful acknowledgement to the EAGLES (Hotel California album released December 8, 1976/ single released February 1977/Grammy Award Record of the Year 1977-reference found on page 4, Illicit Coterie)

Published by Coterie Publishing LLC 2011

Illicit Coterie
ISBN: 0615422268
ISBN-13: 9780615422268
Library of Congress Control Number: 2011925720

First Edition: May 2011
Printed in the United States of America.

Cover design by Elizabeth Renwick

For

Sydnie and Stephanie

My two lovely and exquisitely charming young daughters. Your encouragement, praise and honesty pushed me through while your love, patience and enthusiasm enveloped me. You made being a Mom the best job in the world! And just as I gave you wings to fly, it has been a great honor to watch you use them wisely, soaring to heights I never imagined. I realize now it is time for Mommie to dust off her wings and learn to fly again. Thank you for always having confidence in me and believing that I could soar above the clouds ~ with this novel I have taken flight.

Acknowledgments

With God, all things are possible!

My thanks to

Tony Nizetich

My irreplaceable editor, for a meaningful, collaborative effort. Who knew grammar was so intricate and sometimes complicated? You did! And for that I am most grateful. While by no means did I produce gibberish, it was those nagging little details that just needed to find the right place at the right time. And you did it. Your conscientiousness was beyond compare while working toward a polished product. Thanks, my friend!

My friends for their encouragement

Lisa Behre-Collier	my brother, Steven
Terri Baxter	My "Starbucks Posse"
Jim Murphy	Christy Napier
my niece, Casey	Lisa Osslund
Nichole Coudiere	Chiho Hayakawa
Scott Graven	Dee Dee Bradford
Karrol Baker	Joshua Pena
Lambert Yuen	Wendy Berry

And all my High School and Facebook pals

Alliance

As Marco sat in his plain diminutive car, he wondered just what had caused him to have this ludicrous assignment dumped on him. He began to squirm in the petite and uncomfortable leather seat. He was not built for this type of vehicle; surely his captain knew that. At six-feet-two he found it both agonizing and annoying to have to put up with this. His dark, untamed hair was always brushing against the roof. He knew he must look ridiculous. After finally achieving an agreement between his body and the seat Marco questioned again, *just what have I done this time for the captain to castigate this retribution upon me?* Having been assigned this mundane task, Marco deduced that this was just another sanction imposed against him. He felt the captain had made an example of him and exacted the worst kind of disciplinary action-boring him to death. But Marco was of the belief that neither the execution of his last case nor his performance warranted such punishment. He thought he had done some of his best work to put away some of the worst drug dealers he had seen of late. How could he help it if he accidently arrested an undercover narcotics officer and ruined eight months of his work? Mulling it over he decided to try to justify his actions to himself. But something else was gnawing at Marco. There was another incident which took place during that case which may have tipped the scales against him even further. One of the suspects had gotten the drop on him, knocked him out cold and relieved him of his weapon. And to add further insult, the bastard went on to rob a convenience store down the street with *his* gun while he lay on the ground unconscious. He knew it didn't look good for him, a veteran police officer of eighteen years, but the worst part was it gave the impression he was slipping.

"Let's see," he said to no one; and with that he closed his eyes, lowered himself in his seat and laid his head back on the headrest. Soon he was lost in his thoughts, which swirled like an eddy. Hadn't he worked just a little too hard to end up here? Didn't he close more cases than most of his colleagues? And didn't that earn him the respect he undoubtedly deserved? Yeah, yeah, sometimes there were consequences for his behavior, but didn't he get the bad guys off the streets? Sometimes you just need to act quickly without thinking, or was that react? Whatever, he knew he was good at his job and didn't care what anyone else thought.

In what seemed only moments, a car pulled up behind Marco. He opened his eyes in time to see the lights flash in his rearview mirror. His partner, Frank, had arrived. *None too soon*, thought Marco. Now he could leave and get on with his life. Silly notion though, because Marco knew he didn't really have much of a life outside the police department. That *was* his life and this assignment was getting on his nerves. He found the longer he sat in the car waiting for something to happen - *anything* to happen - the angrier he became. Day after day, hour after hour, minute after minute, tick-tock, tick-tock. Perhaps it was time to have another talk with the captain; for whatever good it would do. But maybe he could finally get the captain to reveal the importance this assignment held, instead of speaking in vague generalities . . . *blah, blah, blah*. Marco needed to make some sense out of this seemingly endless task. He felt his expertise could certainly be put to better use. Exhausted from his thoughts he came back to the reality that he was relieved of duty. He quickly freed his mind, regained his composure, pulled away from the curb and turned at the first corner, away from the street that had been holding him hostage.

Marco began to feel a sense of freedom as he took off toward the police station. He switched on the radio, which was always set to his favorite station. Next, he hit the switch and all the windows came down. His foot pressed the pedal toward the floor, acceleration complete. He turned his attention to the song playing, an oldie from his high school days, resonating from the speakers. He cranked up the volume; "Welcome to the Hotel California, such a lovely place . . ." Marco pushed farther back into his seat as the song played on, ". . . Mirrors on the ceiling and pink champagne on ice, we are all just prisoners here of our own device . . ." He felt like he was soaring through the streets of San Francisco just like he watched on TV when he was a kid. It wasn't until he overshot the station that he realized he had missed it. Oh well, he was feeling better now anyway. He would have that talk with the captain in the morning. He turned left at the next corner and headed toward North Beach. Here, Marco could always find a favorite place, which was nearly anyplace there, to unwind. Best of all, it would seem miles away from the sedate little neighborhood he left behind.

Once Marco reached his intended destination he conveniently confiscated the first parking space he came upon and exited the confines of the car. As he walked, the crisp evening air cleared Marco's head while he reflected on the city's haunting contrasts that could be discovered only blocks apart. He pondered how San Francisco is a city with a multitude of lifestyles flourishing within its boundaries; the fascinating neighborhoods of Nob Hill and the Marina which dropped down into the darkness of the overwhelmed and troubled Tenderloin. How the Financial District appears fortified and formidable against the fury played out in nearby Hunter's Point. And further, how City Hall rests untroubled opposite the park where many homeless take seasonal shelter from the elements. Just as San Francisco owns the difference between land and sea, "The City", as local residents refer to it, holds a reputation for its cosmopolitan air while lending a momentary look at its seedy underside. The belly of The City is where Marco spent most of his time throughout his illustrious police career. He never really got to enjoy the outside until The City was ready to spit him out. That thought brought him back to the present and the realization he had arrived in paradise. Broadway in North Beach was definitely a place to forget all your concerns. Marco walked past all the atypical folks, who if they were anywhere else would be considered unparalleled, even unstable perhaps. But here in North Beach they had sanctuary, a safe haven to play out their inhibitions. Marco ducked into a sidewalk café and grabbed a seat outside on the patio. The climate was moderate but cool, as one might expect on an October night. He was glad he had thrown his favorite red jacket into the car this morning, for it was coming in handy now as the breeze was gently picking up off the bay. No sooner had he settled into his chair he noticed a commotion nearby seemingly caused by an odd little fellow pushing his way through the crush of tables. Marco watched as this character extended his arm and grabbed the chair opposite him. He wasn't of any particular stature, other than the lack of one Marco noted. In fact he was on the short side. Marco finally caught a glimpse of his face when he brushed his out-of-control brown hair aside with his hand.

"Hey, you don't mind me taking this seat do you?" the stranger asked Marco, "it's just that there's no place left to sit. This is the first night off I've had in weeks, and I'd really like to sit and relax awhile. So what do you say?"

Marco began to respond, but this uninvited pest was determined to continue his plea. Marco had no idea he had been pegged for a cop by this pushy intruder.

"You see I've been working on this story for the paper, I work there, and my boss said it would take just a few days to complete. What does *he* know? Anyway, it took me three weeks *and* a few days. Boy, I'm glad it's over though. So, you're not waiting for anyone are you? I wouldn't want to take someone else's seat."

Finally Marco was able to get a word in.

"No I'm not expecting any company. Help yourself. Sit down. Who am I to refuse the freedom of the press?"

The reporter just laughed, "I'm Brody Abernathy, and you are. . . ."

"Marco Morelli."

The two shook hands and then Brody pulled out the empty chair and dropped uncomfortably into it. He leaned forward and looked across the table at Marco. He was ready to put his reporter instincts to work. *I may not be on a story but I'm always on the job,* thought Brody.

"So, Marco, what is it you do for a living? I mean with the way you're acting I'd have to guess you're a cop. You're rigid and seem distracted, a bit too cautious I'd say. But what do *I* know? I'm just a reporter. Maybe my instincts are off tonight," said Brody actually quite sure his instincts were right on.

Marco looked directly back at Brody with a crooked smile. Had he been at this job too long and settled into a false sense of anonymity? He thought surely in North Beach no one would ever pay him any mention. But there he was, this little geek, calling him out. At this point Marco didn't see the harm in coming clean.

"Well good for you. For once the press has it right. I *am* a cop," said Marco.

"I knew it! Not that I had any doubt, mind you, but sometimes I don't get things quite right and I end up paying the consequences. But this is my lucky night!"

Brody was not only elated that he was correct in his assumption, but realized cops are good friends for a reporter to have. He imagined the stories, the scoops, not to mention the bylines and headlines he could get now. He was not going to blow *this* opportunity.

A waitress interrupted Brody's thoughts.

"What will you have, gentlemen?"

Brody looked up at her, and was immediately smitten and ultimately impressed by her appearance. She had the most beautiful flowing blonde hair that appeared as flames when the light danced through its locks. Her tresses framed her face and then drifted down her neck where they came to rest on her shoulders. Her figure was one that most women would contend with, and it rested on the most gifted pair of legs he had ever seen. Brody followed her legs back up to her eyes. They were two lagoons of blue that immersed him until he was swimming in them, mesmerized. Marco rested back in his chair, smiling and watching Brody drool over her. He knew that this was no ordinary woman; she was Sergeant Darcy Barlowe, undercover. It became obvious that Brody's instincts were tipped over by the vision before them. On a good day he would have been suspicious that she was a cop, but today any hints seemed to be immediately overshadowed by his attraction to her.

It was not just by chance that Marco ended up here, it was because of her. He had been trying to get this close to her for months, and when he heard whispers that she was going undercover here, well, he frequented this establishment as much as possible.

Now he found himself trapped at this table with a blathering idiot and would have to put up a contest to get a word in edgewise. Not that he ever really tried before. Marco never really knew how to read her, so he never approached conversation. He resigned himself to engaging in idle chit-chat with her, which never really left him satisfied. He wasn't even sure she knew he was a fellow cop.

"Gentlemen, may I get you something?"

"Sure, bring me a beer, whatever is on tap," Marco stated decisively.

Without even thinking, Brody blurted out, "me too."

Sergeant Barlowe smiled, "I'll be right back." She turned and disappeared among the bustling crowd inside.

"Wow! Did you get a load of that?" Brody panted excitedly, bobbing up and down in his chair trying to follow their 'waitress'.

"A load of what?" Marco queried, toying with him. He was going to have some fun with this.

"That babe. You know, the server, umm waitress, the one who's getting our drinks," Brody heaved a sigh, "she is stunning! I think I'm in love. I am speechless."

Speechless, thought Marco, *that I'd like to see.* But he doubted that would happen any time soon.

A disturbance at the bar inside interrupted Marco's thoughts. He stood up to make way from the patio and enter the establishment when a big husky man with long dark hair ran right into him.

"Hold it! Freeze! Police officer!" The familiar voice of Sergeant Barlowe cut through the air. The broad man regained his footing and took a swing at Marco, but the detective eluded contact. Marco then lunged at the big lug, tackled him and the two went toppling onto a table knocking all its contents into the startled patrons' laps. Soon the crashing of glass was heard as the cups met with the stone tiles below. Everyone outside stood up with excitement and curiosity in time to see the two men land on the ground where Marco wrestled the perpetrator into submission. The man's face was smashed deeply into the unyielding ground while Marco pushed his knee sharply into his back and attempted to grab the flailing arms of his opponent. The aroma of spilt coffee began permeating the air as the struggle continued to captivate the crowd. While everyone around them could be heard laughing and cheering, Sergeant Barlowe steadied her gun on the two men. Brody was aghast and his focus became a laser beam on Barlowe. *How could I have missed this? She's a cop too?* He thought to himself. *You just let a beautiful woman cloud your instincts - never again!* Brody quickly made a mental note to be more careful next time.

He stood up and took in the sight of the two men on the ground with tables and chairs strewn about the patio and onto the sidewalk. Brody suddenly realized he should be taking notes! This was the opportunity he was waiting for, wasn't it?

"I said HOLD IT!" Barlowe resumed, "I'll shoot you - I swear - if you move even one inch. Don't tempt me, either one of you!" Her gaze was fixed upon the two men and the background became a mere shadow of its former self. She was fixated on the matter at hand and ignored the acclamations from the mass of people that now filled the patio. Marco turned and looked her square in the eyes - she wasn't kidding.

He started to reach for his identification, "I'm a cop!" Just then the plentiful fellow quickly rolled over and gave it to Marco square on the chin. Marco held fast, but now he was pissed. He wiped the blood from his lip and then looked directly into the huge guy's face. The hefty man managed to squirm out from under Marco causing the officer to fall backwards onto the ground. Both men managed to stand up and with forcible rage Marco swung and knocked his attacker out cold. His tenacity having paid off, Marco watched as the limp form spun to the side and fell face down onto the patio floor. With a thud the altercation ended.

"Good shot!" Brody excitedly bounced on the sideline closest to the brutal occurrence, raising his fist in victory.

"Stop," Sergeant Barlowe shouted authoritatively as Marco began to put distance between him and the unconscious heap, "where do you think you're going?" Marco turned around to see she was addressing him.

"I, Sergeant Barlowe, am going nowhere." She did not release her stance.

"Ah, so you know who I am, then show me some I.D. I'd like to see if it's true that I have now had my case screwed up by an interfering fellow cop."

Marco reached slowly into his shirt pocket and pulled out his badge and held it out for her.

"Satisfied?" Marco shot sarcastically, "I'm off duty."

Incredulous with his tone, Darcy scrutinized Marco's identification.

"You! Why, Marco Morelli, I have heard about you and your singular style of detective work, but have never had the pleasure of an introduction. Must be my lucky day."

With likewise contempt Marco jerked his identification from her view and shoved it back into his shirt pocket. *What could I ever have seen in her?*

Sergeant Barlowe relaxed her stance and returned her gun to its holster under her shirt. She reached behind her apron and pulled out her handcuffs. She tossed them to Marco, "here, make yourself useful."

As Marco worked to put the cuffs on the *Incredible Hulk*, Barlowe spoke, "you're just full of surprises Morelli."

"Really, you give me too much credit, Barlowe" Marco tossed back.

In order to get closer to the officers, Brody managed to go up against the crush of locals and tourists who had somehow been able to push him aside. Barlowe, recognizing him as Marco's table companion, tossed her head toward him and looked at Marco, "who's your sidekick?"

"He actually doesn't belong to me, he belongs to the press."

"Geez, that's just great," said Barlowe.

"Don't worry," Brody began, "I'll put everything in the best light possible. I mean under the circumstances and all. This will make a credible story. This stuff doesn't happen every day. Well, maybe for you two, but not for me, and I'm sure our readers at the *San Francisco Bay Daily* would like to see this most recent criminal activity in print, whatever it was. So if you. . . ."

"Let's go," Barlowe motioned to Marco, "before he gets us killed or something." Sergeant Barlowe and Marco grabbed up the monstrous suspect and turned toward the street.

"Hey you guys, wait for me," Brody was chasing them, "let me in on this and I won't forget it. We could really help each other. Working the city desk I come across a lot of information that could really be of use to you guys! Roaming the streets is my job, and I'm sure there are some characters that would talk to me that would never talk to you. So, come on, what do you say?" Barlowe and Marco had reached a black and white that was waiting for them around the corner. They struggled getting their huge load into the back. Both turned and looked at Brody who was swiftly trailing behind.

"Would you like to join our companion here?" Sergeant Barlowe asked, motioning to the back seat passenger.

"What for?" Brody stopped abruptly, short of reaching them.

"Let's see," she began, "public nuisance, obstruction. . ." with Marco adding, "interfering with a police investigation."

"Wait a minute. You can't lock me up for any of that, there's no proof I knew anything," Brody beseeched.

"I can and will if you don't stay out of my way," spit the sergeant.

Brody was relentless; "there is no basis for your charges. They won't stick."

"Maybe not, but you sure will be uncomfortable stuck in jail for the hours it takes your paper to bail you out. Now go, or you will be one sorry reporter." Barlowe pushed her way into Brody's personal space. Brody was speechless once more as he watched her turn and head across the street to her car.

Marco leaned over to Brody and winked, "I think she likes you." He laughed as he turned and followed Barlowe, leaving Brody standing on the curb looking like he just saw his dog get run over. Marco felt bad about that, but not that bad.

Once they had reached Sergeant Barlowe's station she had made the decision to let Detective Morelli in on some of the details from the night's excitement - as few as possible. He seemed harmless enough so far, even if he did disrupt her investigation.

Marco interrupted her thoughts, "okay Sarge, you going to fill me in, or what?" He sat down in the chair aside her desk, eased in and put his feet cross-legged on its top.

"Well, I had a mind to, but if you're going to be an ass about this detective. . . ."

"Oooh, ouch, that hurt," he removed his feet from her desk. "Look, all I wanted this evening was a quiet night off," Marco began. "Then along comes 'Clark Kent' who won't shut up, and then you come busting up any possibility of putting another painfully punishing day behind me."

"Boo hoo," the sergeant was unsympathetic, "at least you don't have to stand on your feet night after night wearing these," she kicked her red high-heeled shoes off her overworked and fatigued feet onto the floor before him.

"Alright, but how about this," Marco began, "I'm working on a real yawner. It's a completely pointless assignment with the most irritating partner."

Sergeant Barlowe interrupted leaning toward him, "well at least your partner is still *alive*."

Marco had completely forgotten he had heard something to that effect a while back. But since they worked out of different precincts, details were not readily available to him. He suddenly began to feel sorry for her. His animosity toward her began to fade. He watched as she began to gather folders and papers from her desk without distraction.

Sergeant Barlowe then motioned to a conference room across the hall. "Let's go to the conference room and we can spread out all the information I have so far and maybe you can be of some help, however little that may be." Marco winced at her comment and wondered if his forgiveness was too easily placed.

He followed her into the expansive room and shut the door. In silence she spread out papers, photos and documents.

"Wow," Marco broke the silence, "this must be months of work."

"It is," the sergeant stopped what she was doing and looked thoughtfully at Marco, "this is what got my partner killed."

"And your captain has allowed you to remain on the case? Isn't that a bit unusual?"

"He doesn't know about it yet," she sat down in one of the oversized chairs and put her gaze out the window toward The City, "but I suppose that after tonight, with all that went on, he's bound to get wind of what I'm up to."

Marco lent to pause, and then an idea struck him, "not necessarily."

"What?" The sergeant was already three thoughts ahead and she turned to face Marco.

"Not necessarily," he repeated. "If we put our heads together, surely we can come up with something that will put off the captain, at least for a while longer." Sergeant Barlowe was now eager to have some assistance and was graced with a renewed assurance of hope. Marco queried, "Does your captain have anyone on the case now?"

"Yes. Only he gave it to a couple of undercover detectives from the Special Unit division." She opened a folder and viewed its contents. "That's what really burned me. The captain said it would look less like a vendetta if he let the Special Unit take care of it." She shuffled some papers from inside the folder she was holding as if searching for something important.

"That's *my* division. I wonder who's got the case. Are they having any luck?"

"Who?" Sergeant Barlowe was momentarily preoccupied, "oh, you mean the detectives? That's what I'm looking for. I have someone slip me their reports." She snatched up a paper, "here it is. So far all they've been doing is surveillance on a little house on Fulton Street and have come up with absolutely nothing."

Just then Marco's face could not hide the surprise and recognition of what she had just said.

"What?" She noticed his change in expression. "Do you know something? Tell me." Marco impulsively snatched the paper out of her hand.

"Hey," she tried to grab it back, "this is really important to me. Tell me what you think you know. . . Now!"

Suddenly Marco realized that by some twist of fate he might now begin to understand the scope of his seemingly dreary task. "Remember me saying to you that I am working on a boring assignment?" Sergeant Barlowe nodded affirmatively. "Well, it is doing surveillance on a little house on Fulton Street."

No sooner were the words out of his mouth than she was out of her seat, racing around the broad table to face Marco. "Tell me it isn't so - *Not you!*"

"I'm afraid it is. So maybe now we can help each other out." The sergeant leaned over the table and rapidly began scooping up the papers. Marco grabbed her arm and the papers scattered, floating to resting places all over the room. As he turned her to face him he noticed pools of unfallen tears in her eyes.

"Look," Marco lowered his tone, "maybe we can help each other out." He pulled up a chair and gestured for her to sit down.

"Maybe knowing the importance of my surveillance will help me know just what it is that I am supposed to be looking for. My captain has only told me that this is a sensitive issue and that I am to report anything that goes on at that house." He turned to see that she was following his words, "but the fact is, nothing happens there that I find very interesting, or for that matter, out of place." Marco bent down and began to pick up the papers that had fallen from her arms. He continued, "Maybe you can help shed some light on the facts." Sergeant Barlowe got up, seized a tissue from the box across the room and wiped her eyes.

"I hate this," the sergeant stated, indicating her sudden emotion, "I'm *not* weak, you know, I'm just frustrated. We don't really know *what* we are looking for."

"I didn't take your tears for weakness. You've been through an awful lot lately, and, well, things just haven't been falling into place so neatly."

Barlowe took a deep breath in an attempt to regain her composure, "Exactly. My partner was deep undercover at that house. She was gathering evidence on some sort of consortium, but she wasn't sure what the people were really into, at least that's what she said. I don't think they fully trusted her." She sat down and looked seriously at Marco, "then one night, a few months ago, she phoned me. She was really excited about something. No, not really excited, but worked up, agitated, in a sort of elated way. She said to meet her at the Cliff House later that night and she would fill me in on the 'case of the century'." She paused for another breath to calm herself, "I went to the Cliff House and I waited and waited. She never showed up. I got the feeling that I was being watched. I couldn't be sure because every-one there looked so ordinary, not one person stood out from the crowd." She was slightly more in control now, but the look of bewilderment across her face kept Marco concerned. She continued to gaze in his direction, "the place was packed, which surprised me because there weren't many cars out front. They must have used alternate transportation." She waited for an interruption from Marco, but he held his silence, so she continued, "any-way, most of the people there didn't appear to be locals either. I just had a strange feeling, that's all."

She dropped herself back into the chair, obviously emotionally spent, "so that's all I know. The pieces just don't fit," she confessed with a defeated sigh.

Now it was Marco's turn, "well, from where I stand, you may know more than you think." He paused for a moment and then leaned on the table with his hands and full body weight. "Let me tell you about *my* observations from my investigation." Sergeant Barlowe began to speak, but Marco held up his hand in opposition and balanced himself upright once more.

"See if you can tell me if we're on to something. Every day I watch that house on Fulton Street. I see everyone that comes and goes. They're all very ordinary. Not one person arrives in a vehicle; everyone just walks up to the house. Some arrive at the bus stop nearby. Others come walking up from down the street, so they probably live close by or park somewhere else and walk the rest of the way. They all look benign and plain, kinda boring, that's why sometimes they just lose my attention." Barlowe rolled her eyes, opened her mouth to say something, but Marco wouldn't allow it. He was on a roll.

"Going after these people is quite different from when we chase down obvious criminal types like dope dealers, gang bangers and hookers. Those perpetrators stand out from the crowd; make our job a little easier, so to speak. But the people I'm watching at that house are difficult to profile. They just look like average citizens going about their business. We have trouble following them too. They always move during peak hours when the streets are the busiest, so we lose them. The walls must be reinforced as well because we are unable to use our surveillance equipment to listen in. Either that or they have some sort of scrambling device, who knows. That's the only suspicious thing about them." Not breaking concentration, Marco grabbed the back of the chair and continued, "Telephone lines are useless because they rarely use the phone. And when they do, it's just small talk." He paused for a moment to grab a soda from the counter nearby, popped the top and took a long sip. He offered some to the sergeant, but she just motioned for him to continue. She leaned back in her chair and crossed her arms. She was slightly captivated now, but still not certain of Marco.

"From the outside it seems like an ordinary house with ordinary people coming and going. But after hearing what you have told me, my instincts say that all this points to the contrary. There seems to be no laws being broken, so we can't make a move on them just because they are *ordinary*." He sat down and leaned across the table toward her, "so, maybe if we join forces, carefully go over every fact, maybe we can come up with an idea of what's going on in that house." After a short pause, Sergeant Barlowe rose from her seat, walked over to the table in the corner and picked up the phone.

"There's just one thing you had better do before we get started," she held out the receiver to him, "call that newspaper friend of yours and tell him not to run a story on what happened tonight. That guy you tackled at the café is a link, albeit a weak one, to this case. To run a story now would ruin any chance of getting him to cooperate." Marco rose from his chair, walked over to the sergeant, grasped the phone from her and returned it to its settled position.

"Hey," Sergeant Barlowe started to reach for the phone but Marco stepped in the way.

"How about this," he looked directly into her eyes - up close. For a moment he thought he would get lost in her gaze. Quickly he turned, took a breath and regained his composure.

"What if we get this newspaper guy, who by the way has the unfortunate luck of being named Brody Abernathy, on our side? I tell him not to print a story in exchange for an exclusive when this case is solved." Marco turned back to face her. She did not look at all pleased with his idea.

"You're kidding, right? Do you think he'll just pass up a byline so that we can do our jobs? I don't think so. He'll just get in the way." She got up in Marco's face, "you saw him, all over us at the café, following us with the suspect, begging for an interview. . . ." Marco just stood there and took it.

"No, I'm banking that he won't," he made his voice low and deliberate. "Don't you remember what he said? 'I can get people to talk to me that won't talk to you.' Don't you see? It would be perfect. We could use this guy to get information from some of the people visiting that house that we could never think of getting close to. Or maybe he even knows of other contacts that could help move this case along. C'mon, what do ya say?"

"Oh alright, but he will be expecting us to give him something in return, something more immediate." Marco knew she was right. Brody *was* persistent.

"So, we feed him tidbits; some unimportant details. Which, if revealed, will help move our case along, see?"

"Okay, I sure hope you know what you're doing." The sergeant resigned herself to the idea, but she was going to keep a close eye on Marco just in case.

"So do I."

୧୭

Marco picked up the phone and dialed information. They connected him with the number and Marco requested Brody's extension.

"City desk. Abernathy here. How can you help me?" came the voice at the other end of the line.

"Hey, Brody, this is Marco, the cop. Remember me from earlier this evening?"

"Hey buddy, I sure do. Are you ready to give up some details on what went down? You're not gonna screw with me are ya? And how about cop chick, does she remember me?"

"I'm not exactly ready to give you any details or answers just yet. Really, we don't have much ourselves." Marco winked at Barlowe who just rolled her eyes at him and turned to look out the window once again.

"Wait a minute," Brody was disappointed, "don't hold out on me now. I know you must have *something*, anything. . . I saw what happened, I was there, remember? That was a whole lot of something to be nothing! You know I can get this put together without your help, it's just that I'll have to do the digging myself, that's all."

"Listen, Brody," Marco began, "I would give you more if I could, but you have to understand that tonight was just the tip of something much bigger."

"*Bigger?* Marco, tell me. I have to know!"

"Look, Brody, it's got to be this way. I give you what I can and you will just have to trust me. It's really not safe to talk about things right now. There, I've said too much already," Marco teased.

"But. . . ."

"At the same time, however, I have to be able to trust you to get me the information you promised, understand?"

"Sure, but. . . ."

"Here's where we stand right now: Sergeant Barlowe, whom you adoringly refer to as 'cop chick' has agreed to work with you," Marco could feel a cold, steel glare fixate on him from across the room, "ironically she has been working on the same case I have, only from another angle, see? That guy that I took down tonight has something to do with the case, and so far he is the only link we have in solving it."

"I guess I'm not following you. What aren't you telling me?" Brody was tired now and feeling it, and Marco was just exasperating him. He dropped his head on his desk, holding firmly to the receiver.

"Brody, I didn't say I wasn't going to give you *any* information. I'm trying to tell you that I *can't* reveal anything about what went down tonight. However, I'm going to make a deal with you if you can accept that."

Brody raised his head from his desk, rested his chin on his palm and took in a big breath, "okay, so what if I do? What's in it for me?"

"That's better." Marco continued, "I'll give you information during the course of this investigation so you can have your story. When Sergeant Barlowe and I come across any breakthroughs, we'll keep you informed. You'll need to take this information and try and mete out anything further from your contacts, see? Trust me, pal, this is going to be something bigger than just some random guy in a café in North Beach."

"Alright, let's say that I trust you to do this for me, what's to say that you and cop chick aren't trying to jerk me around and stall my efforts?"

"Look, this partnership, as such, will benefit both sides. By giving you certain details to report on in the newspaper, perhaps we can make some people nervous enough to make mistakes. You see, so far it appears that there is a group of people so clever that no one has been able to even discover who they are and what they're up to . . . *yet*."

"Now this sounds like we're getting somewhere. What group of people are you talking about? Where are they? Here? What evidence do you have on them so far? What am I going to print tomorrow?"

"First, you can do a story on Sergeant Barlowe's ex-partner. It's believed that she was killed while investigating this case. They never recovered her body, so that's a little suspicious in itself. Dig up some information on her, you know, the usual stuff on her past, her time serving as an officer, what led up to her possible demise and anything else you can find regarding her death. That ought to get someone nervous enough to make a mistake." Marco waited for Brody to interject, but found him to be uncharacteristically quiet, so he continued.

"I'll fax you what details I can from the department and you can start some background research on her." Marco searched the table and found the paper describing the slain officer's information.

"In the meantime, her name is Detective Angela Paxton. She lived in the Richmond District. She was born in San Francisco on July 4, 1962. Anything further on her police career, I will send you. That should be enough to get you started. Oh, and really look hard into her death. We don't seem to have much to go on; maybe you'll have better luck. If you have any questions about her personal life, you might want to ask Sergeant Barlowe, she'll be waiting to hear from you." Barlowe stared in his direction.

"I'll get on this first thing tomorrow. I'm beat and could sure use a shower and some sleep."

"Sleep? I thought you were a professional?" Marco laughed tauntingly into the phone.

"Very funny. Hanging up now. Call me tomorrow." Brody yawned, dropped the phone into place and put his head on his folded arms across his desk and was asleep before he knew it.

Barlowe watched as Marco returned the phone to its resting place.

"You know, detective, this is still my case. I don't know if I like you taking over like this."

"Hey, wait a minute. You wouldn't have a case, *officially*, if it weren't for me. Your captain doesn't even know what you're up to. Do you think you can avoid him forever?" Marco was feeling quite pleased with himself as usual. "You should be thankful that I'm willing to let you work with *me*." Sergeant Barlowe was on her feet with newfound strength.

"*Thankful!*" Thankful for you getting in the way of *my* investigation?"

"Wait a minute," Marco put out his hand in a calming gesture, "do you want your captain to find out in the morning what you've really been doing? He would kick you off the case *and* kick your ass. Probably hand you a suspension as a reward, too. On the other hand, you now have me."

"Ooooh," she rolled her eyes and sat back down in a heap. Marco ignored the response.

"Who better than the detective in charge of the investigation to have on your side? You won't lose any ground or sleep over this. I have my partner, Frank, watching the house at this very moment. During the day, it is my pleasure to sit there hour after hour watching nothing. It will be to my benefit to have you here searching files and records. Maybe you would have better luck following some of these people too. I think Frank and I have been burned anyway. They've got to know we've been running surveillance on them these past few weeks. And now we have a newspaper guy on our side. So, what do you say?" He leaned on the table and looked directly into her eyes.

"And even if it comes to your captain finding out, take the tongue-lashing from him; go along with anything he recommends. Be the model officer and be secure in the knowledge that you haven't had to give up anything in this investigation." Marco wrapped up his proposition and waited for a response.

"If I do as you say, do you swear that I will be just as involved as I am now?"

"More. You will have plenty of work here, because Frank and I will be down by the house. Maybe you can even spend some time there as well. We can all gather pieces of the puzzle and assemble them together."

"Okay, then let's get through all this information so we can bring each other up to speed." Barlowe took a moment, paced, took a deep breath and sighed.

"Let's do it." Spending the night with Sergeant Barlowe was definitely not a hardship; only problem was that they were working.

It was nearing three in the morning before the two of them remembered that they still had the perp in a holding cell. They both agreed that they had better get some answers from him before the captain found out and ordered him released. Sergeant Barlowe called down to holding and told them to move the guy up to an interrogation room. She and Detective Morelli gathered the papers and files from the table and headed down the hall to get some answers. As they entered the room, they saw their big catch sitting in the chair smoking a cigarette, remarkably calm. Marco finally got to take a good look at this tough-acting dude.

He was enormous, not just in stature, but in bulk. His face was repulsive and hideous, partially shadowed by a couple days' growth of stubble. He also had long, stringy dark hair partially covering his dark, frightening eyes, which revealed defiance. He had on a sleeveless black t-shirt showing off his many tattoos; a dying woman with a knife in her chest, a snake wrapped around a man squeezing the life out of him with eyes bulging and others depicting various reptiles. The one that caught Marco's eye though was the one at the top of his left shoulder reading simply *MOM*. Marco's observations were interrupted when their prisoner spoke.

"So what's the problem with you two anyway? Why are you screwing up my life?"

Sergeant Barlowe sat down across the table from him while Marco remained standing near the door. Marco wanted to watch how the sergeant was going to carry out the interrogation. He figured he was much more capable of handling the extraction of information from the cocky ass than she was but he decided to stand back and let her have a go at him.

"Let's see here," Sergeant Barlowe picked up a piece of paper and steadied her eyes on it.

"According to your fingerprints it shows here that you are one Thomas James Schultz." She continued, never letting her eyes up from the paper, "you have had numerous arrests in Louisiana before deciding to share your creativity with our city."

"Yeah, so I've made a couple of mistakes. What of it? You got nothin' on me now, do ya?" He snorted, "So why don't you cut the crap, huh, and let me go?"

"*A couple of mistakes?*" She returned with incredulousness. "Says here that you've been quite a busy little beaver here in our town, Mr. Schultz. Lately you've been lifting computers, printers, cell phones and even attempted satellite dishes. If I may say so, and no insult intended, I assure you, you just don't seem like the kind of guy that would be into stealing things of a technological value." He straightened himself up in his chair and cruelly snuffed out his cigarette.

"Is that so?" With this the sergeant put the paper down and looked him in the eyes.

"What gives, Mr. Schultz? Who are you working for? And why did you run from me last night?"

"First, I was running because you grabbed my arm, you crazy bitch. I saw the expression on your face and wasn't gonna stick around to find out what you wanted; I've seen that look before." Marco waited for her to respond but Barlowe sat stoically listening.

"And what makes you think I just don't find this stuff interesting? Besides that the resale value on all that high-tech shit gets me a good return on my investment. Wouldn't you say? And why do you think I am working for anyone, huh? I am an entrepreneur. I am my own boss. Like I said, you got nothin'. So why don't you be a nice lady cop and let me go?" He leaned back in his seat and folded his hands behind his head. Just when Marco was about to step in and try his luck, Sergeant Barlowe was on her feet. She slammed her hands down on the table and looked directly into Thomas Schultz's eyes.

"Look, either you tell us what you're *really* up to or I will put the word out that you told us anyway."

"Oh wow, is this *you* getting tough on *me*?" He removed his clasped hands and put them on the table leaning closer to the sergeant. "Is that supposed to scare me into submission?" Feeling she was getting nowhere, the sergeant lifted her hands from the table, stood erect and motioned toward the door.

"If that's the way you want to play, so be it. You, Mr. Schultz are free to go. But remember that from now on you will have us on your back. You will have everyone out there on the street wondering if you snitched. You won't be worth the junk you steal because now no one will want to touch you ever again."

"We'll just see about that." Thomas Schultz snatched his pack of cigarettes from the table, pushed Marco aside and walked out the door to freedom. As soon as he was out in the hallway, Marco slammed the door shut.

"Now what in the hell are we supposed to do? You just let our best and only lead get away." Sergeant Barlowe remained calm at his outburst. She knew what she was doing, even if he didn't.

"I just used a little street psychology, that's all. I learned it from my partner. You see, I planted a seed in his itty-bitty but arrogant little mind by telling him that he won't be able to unload any further stolen goods. But if my guess is right, he will still try anyway. It's just that now he'll try sooner than later."

"That sounds great in theory, and I've tried it myself from time to time with little or no results, but if you believe it will work, then I'll go along. So who's going to follow him?"

She glanced at her watch and back at Marco, "why *we* are detective." She grabbed the stack of files, opened the door and was halfway down the hall when she realized Marco was not behind her.

"Hey, detective," she shouted, "are you coming or not? Let's go!" Marco quickened his pace to catch up to her.

"We'll take the side exit and wait for him on the street." And with that she kicked open the door and walked out into the darkness.

Marco glanced at his watch now illuminated by the streetlight. It was a quarter to four in the morning. A chill came over him. He zipped up his jacket and thought to himself, *so much for a nice evening with a beautiful woman, so much for even considering sleep, so much for even considering having a life of my own.*

They were standing behind the corner of the building when Thomas Schultz came bursting out the precinct door and down the stairs to the sidewalk. He slowed his pace to light a cigarette and then set off down the street toward them. The two ducked behind a patrol car as he walked by, holding their breath and their futures on the line. As soon as he had passed a safe distance, Sergeant Barlowe motioned to Marco to follow her to her car in the precinct lot. Carefully she opened the door without a sound and got in, tossing the files in the back seat. Marco stealthily entered the passenger side. They pulled out of the parking lot and onto the street. Mr. Schultz was then observed walking slowly and deliberately, block after block. He appeared as a mere silhouette against a backdrop lit only by city lights. The two let him get ahead a few blocks at a time, moving the car and parking to continue their surveillance.

"This isn't getting us anywhere," said Marco, breaking the silence. "This guy's not going to make any moves now. He's going home to a hot shower and bed, which is where I'd like to be about now."

"Get serious. Did he look like the type that was concerned with any kind of personal hygiene? So far Mr. Schultz has wasted a night with us and has not been able to swing a profit yet. I'd bet right now he is actually casing these businesses to see if one may be of interest to him. He's probably just waiting until he's far enough from the station."

"If you say so." Marco slid down in his seat and laid his head on the headrest; her actions reminiscent of his long days of surveillance. "You seem to know what's going on. Wake me when something happens, I'd sure hate to miss anything." And with that he closed his eyes, begging for a moment of sleep to take him.

The sergeant kept her eyes on Mr. Schultz, following his every move, trying to get into his thoughts. She broke her concentration for a moment when two figures stepped from the shadows underneath a broken streetlight just ahead of him. She wished she had a clearer view. She glanced across back at Schultz. He seemed unalarmed and even quickened his pace toward them. Sergeant Barlowe's pulse quickened, her breath accelerated and then she backhanded Marco.

"Wake up, something's going down."

"You must be imagining things," he said as he slid up in the seat, rubbing his eyes.

"No, really," her voice was intonating excitement, "look up there. See them? Two strangers just joined the party." She pointed at the two shadows and Thomas Schultz. Marco's eyes came into focus and zeroed in on the two figures in time to see a third form step from the shadows just as Schultz had reached them. He noticed that Schultz became instantly rigid.

"What's that about? He seemed in an all-fired up rush to get to the other side of the street and then . . . what happened?" Marco inquired.

"Well it certainly isn't anything I was counting on. I wonder why that third guy caused Schultz to stop dead in his tracks." Her eyes remained fixed on the scene ahead. "Can you see what's happening?"

"It seems like you're doing just fine with your play-by-play account of the situation." Marco looked over at her, "am I wrong?"

"That was rhetorical, you know, not requiring a response."

"I know that."

"Can you maintain focus for once? We've got a job to do and by some sick twist of fate I'm stuck here with you." Just then a shot rang out and echoed past them. Both officers strained to look through the lightly misted windshield and saw nothing but a huddled mound lying near the gutter where Thomas Schultz had once stood. Nothing more. No dark figures. No other sounds.

Sergeant Barlowe instinctively turned the key in the ignition. Just as she was pulling away from the curb and was gaining speed, a sanitation truck drove out from an alley preventing their advancement. The sergeant immediately slammed on the brakes so hard it forced all the car's contents to be redirected forward. Marco braced for impact, but Barlowe's car still had several feet of clearance.

"That was close," said Marco.

"That truck just came out of nowhere. I wish he'd get out of the way."

They waited for a moment to see if the truck was going to move.

"I'm going to go tell that driver he's interfering with a police investigation and he should. . . ." Just as Marco opened his door, the truck began to move forward.

"Get back in. Hurry up!"

Marco threw himself back into the car and slammed the door shut. They had lost sight of Thomas Schultz and the shadowy figures that were now on the other side of the temporary roadblock which impeded their progress forward. Both of them were anxious to find out what was happening with the suspects. The truck moved past where the figures once stood and they could now see its brake lights piercing the darkness. Sergeant Barlowe accelerated cautiously toward the scene, unsure of what to expect. What she hadn't counted on was another vehicle. A car had turned out of the same alley where the dark figures had once been and was heading directly toward them. As it got closer Darcy could see the windows on the car were rolled down and a man in a hat was in the back seat leaning out drawing a weapon on them. She quickly pulled her car up to the curb and stopped.

"Get out!" she screamed. Marco opened the passenger door and slid out, the sergeant followed behind. They crouched behind her car waiting, realizing they were now in dire straits. As the car passed them a hail of bullets was unleashed in their direction. An instant combination of glass breaking, bullets piercing the vehicle and ricocheting off the building together with the pounding of their own heartbeats caused an acute adrenaline rush. When the onslaught ended, they rose from their positions, pistols poised, but they were too late. The car had turned off the street and was well away.

They turned their attention back up the street where they last spotted Mr. Schultz. They were surprised to see two men exit the sanitation truck and approach the heap, which the officers contended was Mr. Schultz. They then watched as the men picked him up and threw him into the bin at the rear of the truck, get back inside and drive away from them, turning at the other end of the street.

"Well, what do you want to do now?" inquired Marco as he released his stance and returned his gun to its rightful place alongside him. He then looked back toward Darcy, waiting for a response.

"Seeing as we just let our only suspect get himself whacked and nearly getting ourselves shot up in the process, I think that's good enough for one night's work."

"Not to mention all the fun we had in North Beach. Yeah, we've had our fill of action this evening even though we still lack any hard evidence. It seems very strange to me that while you're following up on your partner's murder and I'm watching some boring little house, we discover there's some connection, but what? And while we pull this dope in off the streets it nearly costs us our careers . . . as well as our lives."

"After what just happened out here, you can bet I'm going to dig deeper to find out what we're up against." With that the sergeant turned toward her car. All hopes momentarily dashed when she saw the damage that had been inflicted upon it. Marco watched her deflate.

"Hey, what do you care about this car? We'll just call in for a tow and get another one."

"You don't understand, this is *my* car," she went over and kicked its side in frustration, "I just paid it off last month." She turned back to him, her arms straight at her sides in momentary defeat.

"We're going to get these bastards if it takes every last breath I have," Darcy promised.

"It just may," Marco replied. He walked over and took the gun from her clenched fingers.

"Let's just leave the car here for now," Marco put his arm around her, but only as a gesture of support he convinced himself. "I know a place not far from here where we can get some breakfast." Sergeant Barlowe did not say a word, but went along with Detective Morelli's lead. He knew she was down for the moment, but certainly not out.

Instinct

As Marco began to stir he felt a cool wetness pass across his cheek. Some misplaced locks were brushed gently off his brow. Fighting through the slumbering haze he felt his arm being rubbed slowly, stroked over and again. Marco was closing in on consciousness and he was now aware of a heavy touch journeying from his chest to parts unknown. He raised his arms over his head extending them into a serious stretch and pushed out a moaning sigh. Marco opened his eyes.

"*Bullet!*" His voice pierced the silence. The cat, taken unawares, instinctively sprang straight up as if naturally catapulted. Immediately gravity landed her directly on Marco's midsection. Her green eyes became alert and protruding, her tiny heartbeat quickened. The excitement of the outburst made her claws extend deeply into the mass below, forcing her to hold on for her life. The sensation of the penetrating sting caused Marco to recoil from the malaise. Relinquished silver fur floated through the sunlight beaming in from the nearby bay window. Just then the phone rang causing both cat and man to be unexpectedly startled. Marco grabbed the nearest edge of his oversized comforter and sprung the cat airborne. She landed cleanly and precisely just inside the bedroom doorway and without looking back, raced off, her pads slamming at a rapid pace on the hardwood floor. The phone was on its third ring before Marco grabbed up the receiver.

"*What is it!*" his voice split through the line.

"Geez, what's up your ass this morning?" came Frank's familiar voice; "I should be the cranky one seeing you should've been here to relieve me over half an hour ago."

"Crap," Marco began, his clarity completely regained. "Hey man, give me an hour and I'll meet you. I've got a lead on our case you won't believe."

"Get serious. We've been wasting our time for weeks being tortured out here and nothing. . . ." Marco cut him off.

"Look, do you remember the place we used to meet when we were working on the Pemberton case?"

"Yeah, but. . . ."

"Don't say anything more. Just take off for there now and make sure you're not followed."

"Sure. And hey, you sound a little out of breath. Did I interrupt you? Were you in the middle of something?" Frank let out an evil laugh.

"Sure," Marco smiled playing along, "just grabbing a little pussy this morning." He hung up the phone and went to look for Bullet to make up with her for the early morning jump-start.

An hour later, Marco was making the turn off the Golden Gate Bridge to Sausalito. The road curved back around and he found himself facing the bridge. He always appreciated the way the clouds rested atop the awesome span, and how the girders rose up into the mist and disappeared into the warm glow of the morning sun. The soothing sound of the waves lapped upon the rocks as the fierce ocean retreated into the horizon. Marco made another turn toward waters' edge.

There was Frank standing alongside his car looking at his watch, something he'd gotten in the bad habit of doing since being assigned this case. Marco pulled up near Frank's car and got out. Frank hurriedly approached Marco in an attempt to get this over with. He had been up all night and the last thing he felt up for was any drama. But this was his partner of seven years, and Marco would have done the same if the request were made of him. Frank prepared himself to listen to whatever it was that Marco so urgently needed to tell him.

As he got closer to Marco, Frank noticed the serious look on Marco's face - a look he had not seen in years. He watched carefully as Marco paused for a moment to look back at the bridge. His dark hair became instantly unmanageable as the force of the cool ocean breeze tossed each lock out of place. Frank smiled at the way Marco's shirt hugged his tight muscular form. *Apparently*, Frank thought, *those nights at the gym have paid off fabulously. And those jeans, really emphasized. . . .*

"Hey Frank," his thoughts were interrupted, "sorry about this morning, but you just won't believe what I've found out." Frank broke his gaze and reached nervously in his back pocket for his cigarettes, embarrassed for his thoughts even after all these years.

"Last night I went to North Beach to grab some coffee," Marco began as Frank lit his cigarette and regained his composure. "I was just settling in when this crazy reporter, a perp and Sergeant Barlowe interrupted a perfectly good evening." Marco then continued with the complete tale of the events from the night before.

"Holy shit!" Exclaimed Frank, "I don't know what to think about all this now. Geez, we could be sitting on the top of some sort of iceberg or something."

"And we're going to need a bonfire to thaw through this mess."

"Now I'm excited!" Frank was pacing wildly, cigarette ashes blowing everywhere as his arms exclaimed his gusto. "Do you realize the potential?" Marco calmly nodded back. One drama queen was enough.

"Oh my God, what's next?" Frank asked, suddenly stopping in place waiting for Marco's controlled direction.

"OK, here's what I need you to do. After you get some rest. . . ."

"Can't do that now - I'm too worked up," Frank interrupted.

"You're going to have to because I need you in top form. We're going to have to be extremely cautious and plugged in with this one. Don't forget about Sergeant Barlowe's partner – dead."

"OK, deep breath, focus, Zen, center . . . ." Marco rolled his eyes outside Frank's view. He may be a little off, thought Marco, but Frank was the best friend and partner he'd ever known.

"Why don't you, *after some rest*, hit the streets and check out anything odd that your contacts have noticed. Hang back secretly and see what slithers out."

"Sure, I can do that," Frank agreed.

"I'm going over to the paper to see if Brody has come up with anything on Darcy's, I mean, Sergeant Barlowe's partner." Frank suddenly felt a sting as Marco spoke with newfound familiarity toward Sergeant Barlowe. He knew Marco had "a thing" for her, but now they were getting all tangled up. *I can handle it*, he told himself, *as long as she doesn't get in the way*.

"OK, but who's going to watch the house?" asked Frank.

"I've got that covered. I called Sergeant Barlowe and she's going to try to follow some of those strange little people."

"What about. . . ."

"Don't worry," Marco reassured, "everything is covered. No one will be the wiser. Not even Captain Dupree." The captain these days seemed more interested in playing it safe (riding out his days until retirement) than truly getting involved. Marco felt assured as long as nothing went awry with his plan.

"I hope you're right," said Frank. The two men then slapped each other's forearms and nodded. They walked away in silence and then purposefully boarded their respective vehicles and raced off back over the bridge to The City.

ᘒ

Sergeant Barlowe sat nervously at her desk in the squad room. She looked up at the sterile, generic wall clock and noticed she was late getting to Fulton Street, but she needed to grab her notes first. Underneath her day's reports were the folders that held potential clues. The collection of innuendos and observances were ambiguous and seemingly unrelated. The unearthed and devastating events of the previous night were so clear in her mind that she jumped when she heard her captain throw a logbook the distance of the squad room. She looked up in time to see two detectives run past her desk in a panic as if their lives depended on it. One of them stopped to pick up the logbook and they both continued on in one fluid movement down the stairs.

"*Barlowe!*" The captain's harsh, unsympathetic voice shot from his office. "Get in here, NOW!" She turned in his direction in time to see him kick a chair across the open door. Captain Morrison was certainly not known for his pleasant demeanor or tactful manner, but this was definitely over the top, even for him. Darcy quickly scanned the room for sympathetic eyes, but none were to be found. Everyone seemed to have found something to bury their heads in. *Chickens*, she thought. *Oh well, better get this over with.* And with that disconcerting notion, she reluctantly headed toward the captain's office.

"Shut the door," he commanded, "and don't bother sitting down." Not that she could since she observed the mistreated chair had been wedged between the filing cabinet and the side edge of the bookcase.

She turned her attention back to the captain, her gaze fixed on his cold, hard stare. He was just a little older than she, but the years had not been a friend to him. The captain furrowed his untamed brows, which were in stark contrast with his short cut, slicked-back ebony hair. He leaned forward and rested his elbows on his desk allowing his midriff protrusion to sink below its edge.

"What's this I hear about you getting involved in some sort of incident at a coffeehouse out in North Beach? And detaining some bystander and holding him against his will?" Darcy stepped with one foot to the side to maintain her balance. How could he know this, better yet, how *much* does he know? If she came clean with what she already knew he might become completely unglued and take it out on her. He was already pissed off as it was.

"It's really quite by accident, sir, that I became involved."

"So you accidentally tackled a patron and handcuffed him? I can see the misunderstanding in that." His sarcasm was not lost. Caught off guard with that addition, she knew she'd better keep her lies simple and to a minimum so she could better remember them later.

"Oh, that. Well, you see, I first thought there was something wrong when this guy came running out from inside, lost his balance and fell on the patio when he ran into a detective from the SFPD Special Unit." She took a breath not even considering looking directly at the captain. Hell, she barely believed herself so far.

"Anyway, things happened so fast the next thing I remember I was tossing the officer my cuffs." The captain leaned deeply back into his chair; so much that Darcy almost reflexively reached to stop him from tipping over. He swiveled the chair to face the view out the century-old weather-beaten window.

"Go on," he said, this time in monotone.

"Next this detective, Morono, or something like that, told me to help get this guy in for questioning." The captain did not avert his gaze from The City he so loved.

"Now we're getting somewhere."

"Not much happened on my part after that. I went as far as bringing them here because it was closer, and then I went home." Captain Morrison turned only his head to the side and fixed his eyes on Darcy.

"Is that all?" He said, making it clear he knew more.

"Yes sir." She looked directly into his eyes hoping this would be over soon.

"Alright then. Dismissed." Darcy could hardly wait to get out of that room. She hated the position she was now in and further detested how nervous this whole situation was making her. She turned and reached to grab the door handle just as the captain pushed the button on his intercom. The last words she heard as she was exiting were, "Get me Ambrose on the phone, NOW!"

&

Brody felt he had been at his desk long enough. Three cups of coffee made him register a 7.1 on the Richter scale, but keeping quiet about the events of the night before was like magma boiling inside him - waiting to erupt. He grabbed the few notes he was able to write and tucked them in the back of the bottom drawer of his desk and locked it. He glanced around at no one in particular; checking to see if anyone was observing his actions (not that they ever do). Sometimes Brody hated being the owner's nephew. He seemed to have to work twice as hard as anyone else to get his articles in print. No one seemed to take him seriously. And it was all because his uncle, the "Great Bradley Ambrose", did not believe in nepotism - not one bit. In fact Brody sometimes wondered if his uncle even knew he was there at all. But Brody rationalized that running the paper kept his uncle busy enough, even too busy for family. He tried to remember the last time . . . he paused suddenly . . . he didn't have time to put much thought into that now. He was onto something really big. And won't they all be amazed when he's able to steal the other reporters' thunder and finally make a name for himself. Brody abruptly turned his chair, stood up and ran right into Duncan Brewer, one of the senior staff reporters.

"What the hell, Brody, why don't you watch where you're going? Some of us have *real* work to do." Brody turned to respond but Duncan was already cutting a path into the sea of seemingly endless cubicles. Brody just shrugged it off. They were all idiots, and Duncan was the biggest of them all. He would show them up one day, that's for sure, and this case he was working on would be just the thing to do that. He was now provided with a motivation and an inspiration because of Marco. Brody walked through the large smoked glass double doors that led from the main press office, turned and took the stairs down two at a time to the generous wealth of the archives. He had his mission to learn what there was about cop chick's partner, Detective Angela Paxton. He was going to do his part and held on to the hopeful notion that Marco would come through for him.

༄

Marco reached the enormous building of the *San Francisco Bay Daily* by early afternoon. As he stood at the entrance he looked upward and a twinge invited itself on the back of his neck while he strained to catch a glimpse of the gigantically elongated structure. The newspaper's building was one of the tallest in The City. It was built in the shadow of the Bank of America building and its fifty-two stories which stood over it as if to gloat its superiority. Returning his attention to the ornate façade, he chose to allow the doorman to exact an entrance, opposing the more modern automatic turnstile glass doors.

Marco now found himself in the vast reception area. An expansive, semi-circle, black marble desk stood in front of him. The newspaper's logo spread across the front panel. Encasing the wall behind the desk was another logo. This one was quite larger and brighter, graced with an old man's head spinning ridiculously in its center. He found that his hesitation was not to his benefit, as he had to keep dodging the rushing mass of people carrying on about their business. Deciding to forgo the formality of having himself announced, he flashed his detective badge at the stout little fellow behind the reception desk and continued to a bay of elevators just beyond. He then tossed himself into the first arriving elevator and was instantly pressed up against the mirrored panel in the back. *Damn*, he thought, he didn't even know which of the dozens of floors he was supposed to arrive at to find Brody.

As the elevator made its first stop, a mechanical voice announced, "Press Office, Second Floor." Marco watched his window of opportunity fade as he tried in vain to push through the bodies, seemingly of one mass, to no avail.

No one was exiting this floor and the doors appeared to mock him as they slowly closed back into place. The immovable riders in the elevator jeopardized any hope of withdrawal from his confinement. It took three more stops until he could, with an abundance of force get nearer to the doors. He decided that no matter what he would exit at the doors' next release. Suddenly the elevator lunged and seemed to spirit him upward. He looked over at the panel of floors listed next to the doors and read "Express Elevator – from floor 15 to floor 40". Not long after this realization, Marco was suddenly aware that the elevator had stopped with a jolt. Just as quickly, it lowered a couple of feet and came to a halt. Hesitantly the doors opened to reveal that they were not quite aligned with the floor above. Simultaneous groans were heard just before the alarm deafened them all. Marco tried to reach for the emergency phone but a fat-armed man punched his way through the huddled crowd cutting off his attempt. The phone cord disappeared into the group momentarily and was replaced to its position. A man's voice strained to be heard through the piercing sustenance of the alarm.

"It's going to be OK." The man bellowed, "There is someone on the way up to help us. The maintenance engineer is trying to correct the situation."

"I'm not waiting again for this thing," a woman's voice protested with annoyance. "Last time I was stuck for two-and-a-half hours. You can wait, but get me the hell out of here!"

"Calm down," began the slender man closest to the doors, "let's see if we can lift ourselves out on to the floor." And with that, everyone seemed to work in unison, without a word spoken, to get each person elevated and extricated to the freedom of the floor above.

Marco assisted the riders to the fortieth floor and was one of the last people left. The elevator gave a quick jolt down and the exit became instantly smaller. *That couldn't be good*, Marco thought as a new urgency set in. He pushed the heavy man, last other than himself, through the diminishing opening. The man then lay prone on the floor and put forth his outstretched arms for Marco. Marco clenched his hands around each of the man's hands and was pulled to safety. Just then an adjacent elevator door opened and a uniformed man stepped urgently toward them. Suddenly a snap, a bang and a mighty wind could be heard and felt coming from the elevator the group had just exited. The whirring and clamorous sound that followed seemed to get farther and farther away until the elevator's impact sent a concussion that rocked the doors. The uniformed man rushed to a keyhole near the partially opened doors, pushed a key in and turned with all his might. The elevator doors did not seem to want to move, but the man was persistent. He twisted and turned the key until finally the doors obliged, moving to their proper resting position. The force of the trapped wind continued to push through the weak miniscule opening. The doors continued to rattle back and forth and for a second seemed as if they would give in to the intensity pulling from within. In his attempt to withdraw to the stairs along with everyone else, the uniformed man miscalculated his path and fell over an unnoticed potted plant that had been moved during the melee. Marco turned in time to see his head hit flush with the ground and knock him out. He went over to check on the uniformed man's lifeless form and tried to smack him out of his unconsciousness to no avail. Marco looked up and noticed the heavy man had been hesitant in his exit and was observing them. Deciding it wasn't worth trying to carry this guy's dead body weight down forty flights of stairs, Marco motioned for the heavy man to assist in getting the uniformed man off the floor and into the adjacent office. After struggling with the uniformed man they each draped an arm over each of their shoulders and dragged him into the darkened office.

⌒◟◞

Alone in the basement archives, Brody was thrown clear out of his chair. The shock waves from the elevator's forty-story fall had permeated the room with a fierce reckoning. He looked up in time to witness one of the long bookcases tilting away from the wall and aiming directly toward him. He rolled over several times just as it came crashing down beside him. Sparks flew and smoke emanated from the computer as it became crushed under the mass. Dust from the impact of the elevator's landing rushed in from the space under the closed door and rose and swirled around him in large puffs. He was hardly able to see the old wooden door that held him in. Stricken with coughing at every breath he barely found the strength to stand. With each new spasm he felt his energy diminish. Brody grabbed the edge of his un-tucked shirt and covered his nose and mouth. He continued to struggle to his feet with great effort. He promised himself he would not be defeated and continued his insurmountable journey to the door. Without hesitation, and with books and files in continuous motion following gravity to their destinations, Brody painstakingly continued on. The rocking soon relented but not before causing Brody to slip and fall numerous times; his last fall having brought him into direct contact with the handle of the door.

∾

"You idiot!" Bradley Ambrose screamed. "The *last* thing we need is to draw attention to ourselves!" However, truth be told, he was willing to do almost anything for the Fifth Column, but not at the expense of his precious newspaper. The *San Francisco Bay Daily* was his life and meant everything in the world to him. The bulging figure standing at the camera monitors turned and revealed his sheepish grin to Bradley.

"Don't go and get your panties in a bunch. I wouldn't want you suffering one of your panic attacks, not now." It was Captain Morrison, all puffed up with pride over his latest achievement. He never connected any consequences to his own behavior. And witnessing Ambrose's display of weakness over their latest decision was not pleasing to him at all.

"But you don't understand. This was not the time . . . ." Bradley's plea was interrupted.

"This was just the time! Did you not see Detective Morelli get on that elevator?" the Captain shot back. "This was the perfect opportunity to see how good your little contraption works. The deployment was tactically sound; and the result truly more than adequate."

"But really, how many people had to get hurt, or worse, die?" Ambrose droned, "I thought that innocent people were not going to be targeted."

"They were not the target, Morelli was. And did you not expect some collateral damage? You can't be *that* naïve." With that the Captain turned his attention back to the monitors.

"I wish I could see what happened." The Captain was pissed off, banging on the buttons located atop the console. "I thought you had cameras everywhere." He repeatedly changed the viewing angles, rapidly switching from one camera to another. "There's too much dust. I can't see a thing. We're going to have to see that this problem is corrected immediately. Good thing I decided to give this a try, we may not have found out in time about the dust impugning our view and it could have jeopardized the operation."

"Is that all you're worried about? What about my building! What about my nephew? That's just what I need, a dead family member," cried Ambrose in dismay. Even though he was afraid of the Captain he was just a bit more frightened of the situation his counterpart had created.

"Calm down, I'm sure Brody's fine. I'm sure he wasn't anywhere near the shaft. And your building is sound as well," the Captain reassured him. "Besides, the engineer I sent over to rig the elevator affirmed that there would be complete containment within the elevator shaft. Aside from a few fallen books and disheveled desks on the lower levels I'd say everything would have remained in order." Morrison scratched his head, "but what I didn't count on was the seepage of dust. This just has to be dealt with." The captain grabbed his hat with one hand and Bradley's arm with the other and yanked him toward the door.

"Now let's get out of here. Of course we will have to take the elevator." And with that he let out a villainous laugh that made Bradley's hair stand on end.

∽

Marco and the heavy man dragged the uniformed man into the office. His identity became apparent when the patch on the front of his uniform exposed the name, *Winston*. They soon discovered that they weren't alone when they noticed a woman lying in a huddled heap on the floor alongside a desk. The two men tossed their unconscious load onto a nearby sofa across the room in the open waiting area and immediately went over to attend to the woman. Marco shot a glance at the name plate on the desk, *Lulu Tremblay, Executive Secretary*. Just as he turned his attention back to the woman she began to regain her wits and composure.

"Oh my God, what happened?" Lulu inquired of the two men. She tossed her raven hair out of her face to reveal eyes dark as night and cold as ice. She attempted to rise and the two men tried to assist her, but she rebuffed them.

"I can take care of myself, thank you." She stood and held on to the edge of her desk with one hand while she straightened out her skirt and brushed it with the other.

"Are you okay?" inquired the heavy man.

"Of course I am. Can't you see that?" she shot back.

"Geez. It's not like we really care, but you are human after all, aren't you?" retorted Marco.

"Oh please. I don't have time to swap pleasantries with you two, and who is that lump over there on my sofa? Would you remove him please?" With that she stepped back behind her desk and abruptly snatched her handbag. The two men watched her as she came back around and momentarily faced them.

"Don't touch anything. I'm going to the ladies room, and I expect you will all be gone when I return." She raised her chin, turned and walked through the door any-you-please and disappeared down the hallway.

Marco and the heavy man went back to see how Winston was doing. The corner area where the sofa was located was not lighted at the moment. The two of them struggled to see in the darkness, but there was nothing wrong with Marco's hearing when two men's voices seemed to suddenly rise from the inner office, one of which sounded vaguely familiar. The heavy man started to speak, but Marco placed his hand across the man's mouth in an effort to silence him.

∽

Finally having made her way to Fulton Street, Darcy sat hopelessly uncomfortable in the unfamiliar vehicle she had retrieved from impound. A late model domestic sports coup confiscated from yet another of San Francisco's finest. Some student not making the grade at CSUSF decided that it was more lucrative to turn out dope than term papers. So here she is, sitting in some kid's first car that mommy and daddy bought. What must they think of their investment now; the kid *and* the car? She thought back to her first car, a "Beetle". What a slug of a car, at first embarrassing, but when her friends realized how much fun it was to drive in confined spaces, it took on newfound glory. Every alley needed exploring. Every shortcut was revealed, not even the infamous San Francisco taxis could hold a candle to her. Also, racing up the Great Highway past the Cliff House, around Land's End to Baker Beach, the "optional" beach was another adventure. Optional being, *anything goes*; clothing or not, lifestyle alternatives – sex or volleyball, it really was a crazy place. Then, of course, there were the Bay Bridge races to Alameda and back. The only reason she was capable of winning such a feat was because she could slip easily in and out of traffic while still blocking her opponents.

The slamming of a door interrupted her thoughts. She turned her attention toward the shrub-shrouded, eerie, little residence across the street in time to see a man, seemingly lacking years of discretion, rapidly turn off the walkway and head west down the narrow sidewalk. The graceful symmetry of his stature invoked a comparison to a proper English gentleman. His head was held high as if with confidence, his clothing was impeccably put together and he walked with the certainty of an aristocrat. Darcy decided that to follow him in the car would be a bad idea, so she left the shelter of the confines of the vehicle and set out on foot.

It was a brisk afternoon, not uncommon in The City. The wind was blowing easterly and threw open her coat as she headed into it. She clutched at the billowing edges, grabbed on and wrapped her coat and her arms in front of her, holding tight from the intruding wind. She looked up ahead in time to see the gentleman standing at a bus stop greeting the arriving bus. She quickened her pace to cross the street, which caused her heart to do likewise. This is the chance she was waiting for. She was not going to let this opportunity slip through her fingers. Suddenly a gust of wind snarled around her scarf and sent it sailing into the air. Instinctively she reached for it and turned, but it was well on its way overhead. She faced back toward the bus. Darcy didn't notice the worn crevice, otherwise referred to as a "pothole", until she took her next step. It was too late, her foot was swallowed up in it and the rest of her body was instantaneously relieved of forward motion and sent hurling to the ground. As she now found herself sitting in the middle of the street, she pulled her hands up off the pavement and began to brush the asphalt bits from her palms. She saw something to her right and turned to notice it was her scarf landing just a few feet beyond reach. Behind her now she could hear the loud roar of the bus heading off down the street. Laughter overcame her and she closed her eyes and wept out of sheer frustration, imagining what Marco might think of her circumstance. But of course no one ever had to know. How foolish of her. She wasn't telling.

"Excuse me," a deep voice from behind interrupted her dismay, "I believe this is yours." Darcy turned and looked up at the attractive gentleman holding her scarf. *It's him! The man from the house.* Ha, luck was with her after all.

"Why yes. Thank you." Darcy struggled with her balance in an attempt to rise from her predicament. The man held out his sturdy arm for assistance, and she gladly accepted his gesture. Once she was upright, she retrieved her scarf from his outstretched hand and nodded.

"I'm afraid you missed your bus," the man informed her. Darcy looked up to see his dark eyes focused on her and she blushed. This was not like her. But he was displaying attributes quite different from most men she was accustomed to being around.

He took his eyes off her long enough to notice an approaching vehicle. The man gently took the crook of her elbow and guided her to the safety of the sidewalk. *Snap out of it, Darcy,* she thought. *This guy is a potential suspect in what could be the biggest case. . . .*

"There will be another bus in ten minutes. That should provide enough time for the two of us to get acquainted." His voice was like a song. The words just fell together softly and reassuring, likened to an underlying melody. *Darcy, you're not listening. . . .*

"Oh, umm, thank you for picking me up off the street," she averted her gaze and began to brush off her coat with her scarf, "ah, and thanks for getting my scarf back too."

"It was certainly no problem, I assure you. You really should be more careful."

"I know." She felt her senses returning and knew that they would be completely restored as long as she no longer looked at his handsome rugged features.

"I'm new around here and unclear of the bus schedule. I have an appointment to keep, that's why I was in such a rush," Darcy felt the need to explain.

"Well, the buses do run every ten minutes, not to worry." He held out his hand in a gesture of handshake, "my name is Montgomery Stanton."

"I am Darcy Buh," she hesitated, coughed to stall and quickly think of a new last name, "I'm sorry, excuse me. I'm Darcy Baker." And with that they shook on it, coughed on hands and all. If it bothered him, it didn't show.

"So where are you off to Darcy?"

"Oh, a little shopping, Macy's perhaps," she stated matter-of-factly.

"Well, then isn't Macy's the other way?" He pointed back in the direction of the house, "Perhaps you are at the wrong stop."

"No, no I am sure this is it." She paused to formulate an excuse. "Oh, I remember now why I was taking this route. I must have gotten confused after my free-fall. Sorry. I am meeting a friend at the Cliff House for lunch and *then* we are going shopping."

"How coincidental, I am also on my way to the Cliff House."

"Well good then, we can ride together. I see the next bus is just about here."

They stood in silence as the bus pulled up. They boarded and the two chatted about life in The City as the bus rumbled toward the Cliff House. They had commenced an age-old game of cat and mouse, and Darcy was determined to be the cat.

⚬

Frank turned off the Embarcadero and into the parking structure at the Hyatt Regency. He had been given a parking pass from one of his contacts that worked there. He liked the secrecy it afforded because he didn't have to park in designated police parking or randomly on the street. Frank pulled out a tiny notebook from his coat pocket and searched for names of possible contacts. Anyone who might be able to lead him to some answers in this case. Just then his cell phone rang.

"This is Belkin," he declared into the receiver.

"Yes, well you don't know me but I have some information that could be helpful to you," the voice at the other end stated evenly.

"How?"

"I know something about the disappearance of Angela Paxton that I'm sure you will find very interesting."

"I'm sure I would, but how did you know. . . ."

"Never mind, I don't have much time. Can you meet me across from the Federal Treasury building near the cable cars?"

"Sure, but. . . ."

And the call was disconnected.

Frank quickly shoved the notebook back into his pocket and got out of his car and carefully surveyed the area. He observed no one peculiarly lingering in sight. Instinctively he patted his shoulder holster, straightened his leather jacket and closed the car door. Heading toward the exit he drew his arm back and clicked on his car alarm. Frank slid the keys into his pocket and recalled an instance last month when he parked South of Market and wasn't as diligent with turning on his car alarm. He had only been interviewing witnesses for three quarters of an hour when he came back to find the doors wide open and his trunk fully exposed. Oddly enough all his wiring was pulled apart and nothing was actually stolen. At any rate, he hadn't felt like taking the car back to the station with a zillion forms to fill out, so he just took it to one of his buddy's for repairs. No fuss, no muss and all for free.

Frank stepped out of the garage on to Embarcadero and headed north toward Market Street where he was to meet his mysterious informant. He looked up at the clock tower and took note that it was nearing one o'clock. Turning his head to view down Market Street and the Financial District he noticed the lunch hour crush. He saw men and women in business attire clutching papers and brief cases, chattering non-stop most likely about affairs of the job. He always felt sorry for them that their offices always spilled out into the streets and into their lives. The enormous demands placed on them were seriously unfair, not unlike cops. That's why Frank felt he held an enormous empathy for the working people. No wonder gyms were full, doctors' offices were overloaded and shrinks were positively doing a brisk business. Hell, fifty percent of the people he was watching right now were most likely medicated; anti-depressants, high blood pressure, cholesterol and heart medications, all there for the asking. The other fifty percent were probably popping vitamins and sipping herbal remedies to try to detox the stress away. For all that, he was glad his philosophy was not to take anything too seriously, especially his job. Oh, he was excited about this case because he always enjoyed a new adventure, but he felt Marco might be taking its significance far too seriously. Marco was always looking for things that weren't there. And now Marco had Sergeant Barlowe feeding into his frenzy. Frank now felt he was placed in the unlikely position of being the levelheaded one. He laughed out loud at the thought.

Continuing down Market Street, Frank's concentration was broken when a taxi pulled up alongside him. The woman in the back seat was waving her arm motioning for him to come over.

"Are you Frank?" she inquired of him.

Hesitant, Frank looked around and back at the woman, "Yes."

"Then you need to get in. I'm the one who called you. I'm afraid we might be followed and that's why I'm meeting you this way." She opened the door and slid across the seat to allow him in.

As Frank lowered himself into the taxi he thought to himself, *she's as bad as Marco with all this cloak-and-dagger stuff.* Notwithstanding, if this type of behavior continues throughout the investigation he might just have to start taking things more seriously himself. As he closed the door he looked over at the woman to examine her more carefully. She had shoulder-length, dark, wavy hair that was pulled back in a severe manner. She must have felt his gaze for she turned and removed her sunglasses and revealed warm brown eyes set against an olive-skinned canvas. As she smiled at him, Frank noticed movement in his peripheral vision coming from the open car window. Before he could act he heard the crack of his own scull; an explosion illuminated an immense white light, his body went limp and all became darkness. The taxi sped away down Market Street and into the unknowing clamor of business as usual.

⁋

Brody's eyes were still stinging and irritated from the dust that had infiltrated the room, his eyes rejecting the invasion with a waterfall of tears. He was sitting on the floor, leaning against the door. Lifting the edge of his shirt away from his mouth, he wiped at the tears. Blinking to clear his vision, he struggled to focus on the floor and spotted his notes strewn about in front of him. Clinging to the urgency of not being discovered, he crawled on his hands and knees and grabbed every paper he could get his hands on. Satisfied that the retrieval was complete, he surveyed his position once more. The plumes of dust had reduced and settled closer to the floor. The air inside the room was significantly easier to breathe. Brody steadied himself to his feet and turned toward the door. As he twisted the handle and pulled, the glass panel reading Records Room slid from its hold and crashed to bits on the floor in front of him. A small shard had found its way into Brody's leg. The pain was quick and clear, but he knew he had to get out of there swiftly, not only for his own safety but also for the protection of the investigation. No one must find out what he's up to. He reached down to the site of impact on his shin and extricated the glass. Hurriedly he swung the door the rest of the way open, exited the room and turned toward the stairs - miraculously clear - raced to the top, turned and pushed through the doors to the Press Room. Brody was surprised to find Duncan hovering at his desk pacing frantically looking very much like an uncomfortable parrot.

"Oh my God, Brody, are you okay?" Duncan reached and grabbed him by the shoulders.

"What the hell do you care? Afraid I might actually be alive?" Brody stepped back to expel Duncan's grip and in doing so, dropped all his notes.

"Here, let me help you with that." Duncan gestured and leaned in to assist.

"NO!" Brody yelled, almost too forcefully, "I can do this myself."

"Geez, I was only trying to help, you little prick."

"I don't need your help. Never did. Never will." Brody shot back.

As Duncan slowly rose back up he peered at the papers Brody was being so protective of and caught sight of the name, Detective Angela Paxton, *oh shit*. And just when Duncan was about to turn, Brody grabbed a paper titled Fifth Column. *That little turd*, he thought, *is going to get himself in over his head. How could he possibly be smart enough to figure these things out?* Duncan earlier surmised that keeping an eye on Brody was going to be a walk in the park, but now it seems to have turned into an all-out marathon. Duncan raced back to his desk and pushed the speed dial for Bradley Ambrose.

Brody was only momentarily puzzled by Duncan's actions. He had more important a thing to do than wonder what that asshole was up to now. He sat down and began to organize his notes. When he got down to the last few, he didn't recognize them as his but his uncle's. They were on Bradley's letterhead and all contained the title, "Fifth Column." The first page read, "Expenditures on behalf of The Fifth Column." Brody set them aside, not sensing any potential importance to his investigation. He unlocked his desk drawer and placed his notes with the others. A thought occurred to him that perhaps his uncle misplaced these papers and needed them back. He really should take them to him, and while he was there, maybe he could find out what happened to the elevator. The idea was sounding better the more he thought on it, and besides, he hadn't seen his uncle in weeks and was feeling a little neglected. He locked his desk drawer, grabbed his uncle's papers and exited the Press Room making a dash for Bradley's office.

∽

Marco continued to hold his hand tightly on the heavy man's mouth as he watched the two men exit the adjoining office. Marco, frozen, stared intently at them as they abruptly stopped. The smaller man jerked his arm out of the uniformed man's grip.

"Let go of me, Morrison! I can handle myself," Bradley shot.

"I'm not so sure about that."

"Of course I can. I'm not the one who set off the elevator just to elimi-nate one detective at the risk of innocent peoples' lives."

"Don't be so melodramatic Bradley. There are much bigger things at stake here than just you and me. Now get a hold of yourself and let's go." With that the captain grabbed Bradley's arm once again, dragged him across the outer room, through the door and toward the stairs.

Marco stood there with continued motionlessness and did not imme-diately realize that the heavy man had struggled free of his grip. He was brought out of his stupor when Winston, previously unconscious, was try-ing to speak.

"The elevator . . . I'm sorry . . . I had to. . . ." And as if his energy had all been expended, Winston drifted back into a numb mental state.

The heavy man stood up and was gasping for breath, clutching at his throat.

"I'm getting out of here now." He turned, tripped and fell over the coffee table landing sideways on the floor. "This is way over the top. I never expected. . . ."

"Wait," Marco began, "it's too dangerous out there."

"It's too dangerous in here." And with that the man leaned on the table, struggled for balance and disappeared out the door leaving behind a piece of paper that had fallen from his pocket.

Marco walked over and picked it up. It was a business card that read Albert Bouchard, Sr. Executive, San Francisco Bay Daily. Just then a figure appeared in the doorway, not moving. Marco looked into his shocked and bewildered eyes.

"Brody, is that you?"

"Uh huh," came his emotionless response.

"Brody, did you hear all that? Was that your uncle? Did you see the captain?" Not waiting for response he continued, "Did *they* see *you*?"

"Marco? Is that you?" Brody was coming back into the present.

"Yes, buddy. We can't stay here. When they realize I got out of the elevator, I'm in serious trouble."

"I don't think I want to help you anymore, Marco. I just wanted a little fun and lots of acknowledgement."

"Too late, my friend, you're in it now. All the way."

"Oh God, what have I gotten myself into?"

"Snap out of it and grow up Brody. We don't have time for this. Is there another way out of this building?

"Nope."

"Crap."

"There are security cameras everywhere too. We're. . . I mean *you're* dead."

"Not yet." And with that Marco faced Winston, "get over here and help me get this guy out of his clothes."

"I'd love to, but he's not my type." *Brody's himself again*, thought Marco.

"Very funny. Hey, what's that in your hands?" Marco inquired, referring to the papers Brody was clutching.

"Just some notes I found that I think belong to my uncle. I was going to return them to him. I don't know what they are, and in light of what I just overheard, I think I should burn them."

"No way, we're not burning anything. I'll take those for safe keeping." Marco held out his hand to relieve Brody of the documents.

"Gladly." Brody quickly handed the papers over to Marco who tucked them safely inside his jacket, along with Albert's business card. Somehow he felt at that moment as if he was on some kind of scavenger hunt, gathering bits and pieces here and there to win a prize. But what prize? And at what expense?

"C'mon, Brody, get over here and help me get this guy out of his uniform."

Brody assisted Marco in eliminating the man of his clothes. Marco put the jumpsuit on over his clothes and the two men exited the room in silence and made for the bay of elevators. Just then the snooty iceberg of a secretary returned from around the corner. Marco intentionally turned his back to her. Ms. Tremblay, nose in the air, entered the office just as the building lights came back on. The elevator doors opened and Brody and Marco both hesitated before stepping in. Once they entered and as the doors began to close the two men heard Ms. Tremblay shriek. Brody shot out his arm to stop the doors, but Marco deflected it, allowing the doors to close flush. She had undoubtedly discovered the unclothed Winston sprawled out on her lonely sofa. This was Marco's singular enjoyment so far today.

&

There was a lull in conversation between Darcy and her companion, Montgomery, as they reached the next stop. A scrawny young kid boarded the bus, looked around and found an open seat across from Darcy. She studied him. He wore baggy jeans that were hanging down so low it seemed as if gravity was fighting with his belt. His t-shirt was surely from the latest rock group, and his brown stringy hair fell partially over his sunglasses. When he sat down, he shot her a glance, and she could clearly see the piercings through his lip, nose and eyebrow. She smiled and turned back toward Montgomery who was staring out the window. The kid pulled an iPod out of his backpack and turned it on. She could hardly believe how loud the sound was emanating from his earphones; she thought she recognized a haunting melody from Muse. Soon they arrived at another stop and Montgomery checked his watch. Feeling Darcy's eyes on him, he nodded and gave her the most innocent of smiles. *Just remember, Darcy, he's the rat*, the voice in her head reminded her. She returned his smile. They both wanted something from the other and each was determined to obtain it.

∾

"Frank. Frank can you hear me?" the voice was calling urgently, "Detective Belkin, can you hear me? You've had a bad accident. Can you talk to me?"

Frank's conscious self was fighting his unconscious will. The more alert he became, the more aware he was of the pain. He was caught between the warm calm overwhelming him and the sharp coldness of his suffering.

"Frank, you're in the hospital," continued the voice. "Try not to move. We're going to take care of you now."

With that, Frank thought he felt a new twinge of pain in his arm and just as quickly, he was off to a peaceful and painless unconscious state once more.

∾

From the corner of her eye Darcy could see Montgomery check his watch again and reach for a small book from his inside coat pocket. She purposefully dropped her scarf so she could lean over unnoticed to pick it up and perhaps catch a glimpse of the cover. All she could see was the word, Journal. As she rose back up to get comfortable in her seat, he quickly closed the book, returned it to its place and gave her another one of his smiles. This could go on all day, but she was already bored with it. She guessed that's all guys think women need to make them happy, a knowing smile of acknowledgement. *Right*.

Darcy looked up and watched a strange little man and a hard looking woman board the bus. They chose seats nearby. The two of them were discussing the latest news. *Good*, thought Darcy, *at least I'll be able to concentrate on something else other than this awkward silence.*

"Did you hear there was an elevator accident at the *San Francisco Bay Daily* a short time ago?" The woman asked of the man.

"No, what happened?" he asked. Darcy sat up a little straighter, leaning closer to the conversation.

"Well, it seems the elevator broke at the fortieth floor and shot right down to the basement! Miraculously everyone escaped safely. How does that happen?"

"I don't know," replied the man of few words.

"Oh, and they said that a police officer was involved too and that the place is now a dusty mess. You know, I never really trusted the police anyway. I bet they had something to do with this."

"Un-huh."

Darcy's curiosity was getting the best of her. She decided to inquire if the woman had any further details. She leaned over across the aisle and tapped the woman on the shoulder.

"Excuse me," said Darcy and the woman turned to face her, "but do you know anything more about what happened at the newspaper?"

"No I don't. Someone had their radio on at the bus stop and I heard it there. We boarded before I heard anything else. Why?"

"No reason, it's just that I have friends that work there." Darcy was disappointed no further details were forthcoming.

The man finally decided to become an active participant in the conversation by trying to one-up the woman.

"Well did you hear that a police officer was discovered beaten earlier today in the Castro?"

"No I didn't," returned Darcy.

"Justice I say," the woman stated with disgust.

"Not fair woman! They said it looks like the guy's gonna make it. I think they said his name is Frank, you know, just like your favorite cousin," the man said, finally showing some emotion and laughing.

"What are you talking about? Cousin Frank is an idiot."

"Exactly."

Darcy leaned back in her seat unaware Montgomery was observing her. *Could the Frank he mentioned be Marco's partner?* She wondered. *But it's such a common name, probably not. And the accident with the elevator at the newspaper; wasn't Marco going there to check on Brody? I would have heard something from him by now if there was any trouble. But maybe. . . .* Noticing her change in countenance, Montgomery decided to inquire.

"Is anything wrong?"

"No, not really. That conversation just got me to thinking."

"About your friends at the newspaper?"

"Oh, you overheard. Ah, yes, I am a little worried."

"Well, I'm sure they must be fine or someone would have certainly contacted you by now."

"Perhaps you're right. But I feel a little guilty traipsing off to lunch and shopping when they may have been injured." Darcy hoped her ruse would work. She wasn't looking for his permission to leave, but for an *excuse* to leave.

"I suppose I would feel the same if I were to be in your position."

"Then you would find it completely understandable if I left to go find out?"

"Most agreeably so," he returned. Darcy was relieved.

"Then that's what I'll do." She held out her hand to Montgomery, "It's been a pleasure." He took her hand, turned the palm down and brought the back of it to his lips and kissed it. Uncertain of what to do next, Darcy smiled back at him just as the bus came to its next stop. Her scarf slipped to the floor as she retrieved her hand from him. She stood up and was lost in the sea of people exiting.

Montgomery reached down and picked up her elusive scarf. He held it to his face and inhaled her essence. He knew he was on the right track and would pick up her scent another day. Because today, he mused, he had more important business to attend to.

છ્ર

Captain Dupree was at his desk signing off on the latest paperwork from Marco and Frank when an officer came bursting through his office door.

"Captain! It's Frank! Something awful has happened to him and he's in the hospital in really bad shape. Come on, I'll drive you."

Captain Dupree was up so fast that he left his chair spinning in his leave.

∽

Marco exited the elevator two floors before Brody so they wouldn't be seen together. He walked down the remaining two flights using the stairs. Just as he was about to exit the building someone grabbed his arm and pulled him to face them. It was Brody.

"Brody! I thought I. . . ."

"Marco, it's Frank."

"What about Frank?"

"He's been hurt. . . Real bad from what I hear."

"What? How do you know this?"

"I was taking these notes out of my desk," he held them up, "and Duncan, this asshole, comes up to me and says, 'heard about some dumb fag cop got himself all boo-booed in the Castro' and tosses a printout on my desk." Brody held up the copy and Marco's face became red and white all at the same time. He grabbed the paper from Brody's hand but refused to take the time to read it.

"You sure it says Frank?" he asked shaking the paper at Brody.

"Yep, let's go." Brody started for the door.

"Where's he at?"

"San Francisco Memorial. I'll drive."

"No you won't, I'll drive. Now hurry up!" And Marco burst through the door and headed light-speed to his car with Brody on his comet tail.

∽

Frank's mysterious informant turned down an alley in the Tenderloin and parked alongside a large dark sedan. She exited her car and strode around it toward the large man waiting. A cigarette was hanging from her lips on a sunglass-clad countenance; her demeanor indicated she was confident at successfully accomplishing her mission. She was meeting Captain Morrison to get her next assignment. When she had reached him, his outstretched arm swung so furiously that when his hand connected with her cheek it sent her cigarette flying ten feet into some rubbish. A homeless man, spying the prize, picked it up, took a drag and ran off into the shadows with delight.

"Hey, what the hell's that for?" questioned the woman. She rubbed the sting on her cheek with her hand.

"For being an idiot, that's what! Do you realize that now the police are going to be more determined than ever to find out what's going on around here?"

"What the hell, Captain, Frank's out of the picture!"

"Not so fast little girl. He's at the hospital to be sure. But dead? No."

"How can he be at the hospital already? He was on his way out the door when we left him. Alone and no one in sight."

"Can't answer that, but you blew it big time. Now I've got to send someone in to finish the job."

"I'll finish it," she asserted with overconfidence.

"No you won't. I can't compromise you being recognized. Not now. There are cops crawling all over the hospital. I have someone else in mind. He hasn't let me down like this, not yet anyway."

"That will make it even tougher to get to Frank." She wiped the blood from her lip onto her sleeve.

"You just leave that to me."

"Then let me finish," she pleaded.

"Nope, I've got another job for you." Captain Morrison turned to her in all seriousness. "It involves your ex-partner. She's getting too close. I believe she needs to be permanently eliminated. I'm giving you one last chance to get it right." He poked her hard on the shoulder for emphasis, turned and headed toward his car, not leaving her time for comment. "Let me know when it's done," he shouted over his shoulder. And with that he got into his car, closed the door and joined the crush of cars on the one-way street.

Damn, thought Angie, she must have really screwed things up big to be forced to take out her own partner; even though they really weren't partners anymore. Angie thought back to the day they both made detective. They envisioned themselves as a real-life *Cagney & Lacey*. They hung their certificates proudly, Detective Angie Paxton and Detective Darcy Barlowe. The two of them were going to change the world.

Somehow though, things became different when Darcy passed her sergeant's exam. The bitterness crept into the detective-left-behind and continued to grow. Most assuredly that is why she is at this point in her life, Angie thought wistfully. Suddenly she snapped out of it and back to her predicament. The hardness began to return. *I've got a job to do*, she told herself, and she threw herself into her car, slammed it into gear and was off to change the world. Only this time it would be *her* way.

怀	

Marco's car came to a screeching halt in front of the hospital. He threw it into park, pushed open the door and was gone in the split second it took Brody to realize they had arrived. Brody shoved his notes under the seat, slid over to the driver's side, closed the door and headed to find a parking spot. Just then he heard a loud horn honking and some woman yelling at him. The car sped off around him. He drove until he found an open spot and parked. When he got out of Marco's car, he looked around to see who the impatient bitch was. His eyes caught sight of a woman exit her car and close the door with such force that it shook as if in a gale storm. Turning, the woman noticed him staring at her.

"Brody, you idiot! Didn't you see me?"

Oh shit, he thought, *it's cop chick. She must've heard about Frank too. Be sympathetic. Be apologetic. Be nice.* He felt perhaps it would be better if he should be going now.

"Stop right there, Brody. You wait for me," Darcy commanded. Brody froze in place not daring to move.

Darcy caught up to him. "So what do you know? Anything?"

"All I know is Frank's hurt real badly. And Marco just ran up there."

Darcy looked past Brody and was suddenly aware of all the cop cars lined up. She looked back at Brody.

"Let's go." She grabbed onto the sleeve of his jacket and pushed through the doors with Brody along for the ride.

Déjà vu for Brody as the image of the captain pulling his uncle by the arm came to mind.

"Is this how all you guys operate? Enforce your will on everyone?" he asked.

"Not everyone, Brody, just you."

"I'll try to remember that, darling," Brody sarcastically spoke as he batted his lashes at her.

Darcy stopped at the elevator and rolled her eyes. The doors opened and she threw him in first.

"Anything else you have to say newspaper boy?" she spat back at Brody as he was pulling and brushing his hands down his jacket to straighten it out from her manhandling. He looked disdainfully back at her.

"Not a thing." And they rode to the fifth floor in stone cold silence.

The elevator doors opened to reveal a sea of blue uniforms. Darcy grabbed onto Brody once more and began pushing her way to the desk.

"Marco might get mad if I lose you now. And don't even think about taking notes in here. Do you understand?"

"Yes ma'am," Brody stated as he saluted her, behind her back of course.

When they reached the nurse's desk Darcy noticed Marco listening intently to one of the doctors. When they were finished speaking, Marco, having observed the two enter, turned in their direction.

"We need to talk," said Marco.

The mutual silence that followed uncovered what they all felt. This unconventionally aligned group now realized they had stumbled on to a case of grave importance - one that may have cost Frank his life.

Desperate

Frank felt the warmth of the sun on his face as the delicate cool breeze fanned the locks of his sandy hair. He watched the sailboats struggle through the white caps on the bay and was reminded of his own struggles. Deep inside he felt frightened, of what he was not certain. Darkness suddenly fell over him and he sensed the presence of some kind of danger. He endeavored to shake the foreboding feeling rising up inside. The air became frigid and he began to shake. As he turned, a pleasant illumination was revealed to him, piercing the darkness. He felt an overwhelming desire to reach it; he knew somehow it held the answers he was searching for, just waiting to enlighten him. But behind him in the darkness came a familiar voice, of who he could not be sure. The voice was warning him not to be fooled by the light and its promises. He was told to push through the darkness instead; that he had unfinished business and he could not let his team down. Suddenly, with a jolt, he found himself sitting in the stands at a Giants game. He loved baseball. The warmth and the breeze were back now and he settled into a feeling of contentment, a pleasure that usually eluded him. He decided to relax into this newfound drowsy, hazy calm.

"That was close," replied the nurse, holding a set of paddles high in the air. She had been able to return life back to the patient who lay unconscious before her.

"Yep, saved another one," the nearby intern stated matter-of-factly while shutting down the equipment. "So, how about some lunch? I'm starved."

"Sure, but not cafeteria food today. I think I'd like something healthy instead." They both laughed as they retreated into the hallway, their boisterous guffaws echoing into the distance.

∾

Captain Dupree had joined Marco and the others at the hospital desk. Marco was only half listening as the captain droned on seemingly not realizing Frank wasn't just hurt, he was hurt because of what they all were investigating, on what they *shouldn't* be investigating. Or was it that the captain was just sick and tired; sick of the job and tired of having to deal with it. Marco's thoughts returned to Frank and to what happened to him. *What was he doing in the Castro? Who was he meeting there?* Just then Marco noticed the elevator doors open to reveal a familiar face. It was the heavy man he was with in Ambrose's office. He unexpectedly remembered the business card the man left behind in his rush to get away. Marco pulled it out to once again reveal its owner, Albert Bouchard. *Well, Albert, what are you doing here? A coincidence?* He thought not. Marco broke away from the group to go check this guy out. No sooner had he done this, he noticed another familiar face come in to view through the sea of uniforms. It was Ambrose's secretary, Lulu Tremblay. *What are these two up to? This is getting interesting*, Marco thought to himself. He ducked behind a pillar.

Brody noticed Marco's unusual behavior and he scanned the hallway. It was the big guy he saw running from his uncle's office. *What was his name again? Oh yeah, Albert, one of the newspaper's pencil-geeks. And his uncle's secretary. What's this about?* Brody wondered. He turned his head to see Marco emphatically shaking his head in the negative. So, thought Brody, Marco didn't think he was up to investigating; well, he would show him just what he was made of. Ignoring Marco's warning, Brody pushed his way through the crush of officers until he got within earshot of the two conspirators.

"All you have to do is inject this into his I.V. drip." Ms. Tremblay whispered handing a folded cloth to Albert. "Think you can handle this?" She had fixed such a cold stare on the man that it made Brody tremble.

"Sure," he unconvincingly replied. His head was bowed and he was staring at the contents now placed in his hands.

"You better. . . ." Her voice was tight and controlled, "or this will be the last chance for you. Understand?"

"Yes," he looked directly into her eyes and saw that she was serious - dead serious.

"Good." And with that she turned, walked to a waiting elevator and disappeared.

Albert could feel the numbness enveloping his body as he slowly and deliberately pushed through the crowd, helplessly making his way to Frank's room.

As if awakening from the shock of a bad dream, Brody stopped shuddering and bulldozed his way back to Marco, shoving officers aside and ignoring the clamor of their annoyance.

"Marco!" panted Brody. "You've got to get to Frank's room, now!"

"Hold on. Calm down." Marco grabbed hold of Brody.

"No time. They're going to kill him!" Brody said breathlessly.

"What?"

"The big guy, uh, Albert. He has something in his hands and he's going to give it to Frank."

"But Frank's unconscious."

"I know. He's going to inject it into his IV. Go help him!" Brody pleaded pushing him along with urgency.

Marco, having finished processing Brody's monition, quickly turned, rushed over to Sergeant Barlowe and grabbed her arm. Brody leaned over and put his hands on his knees and tried to control his breathing.

"Let's go Darcy. Now! We've got trouble!" The sergeant was momentarily taken aback by the familiar way he addressed her.

"What the hell? Let go of me." Darcy tried to wrestle herself free, but they were already halfway down the hall to Frank's room.

"No time to argue with you. Frank's in trouble!"

Darcy found herself cut loose from Marco's grip but felt compelled to continue on behind him. The two quickly reached the doorway just in time to observe Albert by Frank's bedside, just staring down at him.

"Albert," began Marco, "what's going on?" Darcy shot a glance toward Marco at his recognition of the man before them.

"They want me to kill him. But I just can't. I can't," there was an aching in Albert's voice.

"Then you don't have to," Darcy's voice was calm and motherly as she focused her weapon.

"But if I don't, then I'm dead myself. I can't mess up, not even once. It's an awful mess."

Marco slowly moved around the balding figure and caught a glimpse of the syringe in the bend of Albert's forearm, pressed against his pale skin.

"I just can't do this any longer. I thought I could, the money's good, but I didn't know it would be like this."

Marco shot a glance at Darcy and nodded for her to speak again.

"Listen Albert," she began, "we can help you."

"How? It's too late."

"No. Think about it, we are the only ones here. No one else knows. Let us help you," her reassuring tone was beginning to have an effect on him.

"Are you going to arrest me then? Because I can't let that happen. They'll find a way to kill me. The captain will kill me!"

Darcy shot a glance over at Marco for direction. He was shaking his head side to side.

"No, Albert, we're not going to arrest you, but you'll need to help us though."

"How can I help you? I can't even help myself."

"That's just it. *We* are here to help you, and then *you* can help us in return."

"But. . . ." Just then Marco grabbed hold tight of Albert's arm and snatched the syringe from his hand. Darcy quickly moved in to apprehend Albert, but Marco had already taken control of their suspect. Marco was out of patience and his concentration was solely on making sure Frank was safe. *Screw Albert.* Marco squeezed the contents of the syringe into the sink and disposed of it. Albert just stood there motionless and defeated.

"Let's feed him to the wolves outside," Marco fumed.

"No, Marco, wait," Darcy grabbed hold of Marco's arm, "I have another idea."

"What? This guy just tried to off my partner! I thought if anybody would understand it would be *you*." He was incredulous at the thought of saving this guy.

"Marco, stop, think. We can take him somewhere; someplace safe, away from the police." Marco was pacing now, punching unseen images in the air. Darcy turned her attention to Albert.

"You're going to help us, Albert, aren't you?" She paused to make sure Albert was processing her words. "Look, you don't have any other options here. Either you help us or I will let Marco take you out there to the room full of cops and let them have at you. It's your choice." Albert looked into Darcy's eyes and for just one moment had doubts of which would be his worst fate.

"I think I'll stay with you two."

"Does that mean you'll help us then?" asked Darcy.

"I don't seem to have a choice."

"Just answer her question, asshole!" shouted Marco from across the room.

"Yes. I'll help you," Albert spoke quickly to avoid another affront.

Marco headed across the room to face off with Darcy. This is not at all how he planned on playing the situation.

"I sure hope you know. . . ."

"I'm sure I do." She stepped back into her own space and holstered her weapon.

"Let's get him out of here," ordered Darcy, "I'll go first and you bring him along behind me. Oh, and you might want to lose the jumpsuit too."

Marco stripped off Winston's uniform and deposited it in a nearby laundry bin. Darcy turned, walked down the hall toward the elevator and right into Brody. She started to say something but her voice was disabled by what she saw up ahead. Montgomery Stanton behind the closing doors of the elevator. *What the hell?*

"Hey!" Marco's sidekick broke Darcy's concentration.

"No time for you right now, Brody." She turned to find Marco pulling Albert in tow.

"Change of plans," she said to Marco, "you take him somewhere by yourself. I'm going to Fulton Street. I just had a vision." And with that she rushed to the elevator and began pounding the button as if her life depended on it - and maybe it did.

Brody was unclear of the situation. Should he follow Darcy, who was clearly acting psycho, or rely on his new mentor, Marco, for direction. He chose the latter.

"Hey, Marco, what do you want me to do?"

"Keep working on the story about Barlowe's partner. I just know there's something there, I can feel it."

Hoping to avoid any further contact with his fellow cops, Marco chose to take the stairs instead. With Brody in tow and Albert in a shocked trance, the three of them made their way down the stairs and out to the parking lot. On their way to the car Marco's thoughts turned to the house on Fulton Street. *All the pieces to the puzzle seem to begin and end there. But nothing fits - not yet, anyway.* Marco was determined to find out what keeps leading him back there and Albert was going to help him get some answers. By the time they reached the car it was apparent from Albert's demeanor he was afraid and ashamed at his situation, Brody was clearly out of his element and Marco, well, he was just confused for the moment.

ॐ

Over at Captain Morrison's office, Bradley was nervously pacing.

"This is all too much. Too, too much." Bradley ran his hand over the three hairs left in his comb-over. "My trouble is. . . I should have just said *no.*"

"No to the money or to the power?" Captain Morrison shot back.

"You know what I mean. I mean I didn't mean it."

"For a newspaper guy you sure are frugal with your words."

"Shut up you idiot."

The captain shot out of his chair at this outburst. Bradley stopped pacing, suddenly realizing the impact of his eruption and backed up a safe distance away.

"Whoa, sorry." Bradley held up his hands toward him as if to protect himself from the captain's intimidating advancement. "It's just that my stomach has been bothering me. I think I need a few days away. . . ." he massaged his stomach with his hands.

"What you need is some Pepto and to grow some balls! Got me?" Captain Morrison had little tolerance for indecision and even less for weakness. Unfortunately he found himself aligned with just such a person, but he needed Bradley. The captain surmised that intimidation was clearly not going to work so he decided try another tactic.

"Bradley, my old friend, what I need you to do is stop and think which side you're going to want to be on when this is all over, and who it is that's going to be able to take care of you."

Bradley really wasn't sure he knew *how* he felt, but he sure knew how to respond.

"I get your point. I stand with the Fifth Column of course."

"Good. Good. Now let's get back to business, shall we?"

∾

Marco opened the door to an empty warehouse on the Embarcadero and shoved Albert inside. This was Marco's secret place. No one had knowledge of its existence except for Frank. It was a safe place for them when they needed it. No one was the wiser, not even their captain. Many times they had hidden out there, out of range from Dupree's rage, and bided their time until he had a chance to cool off and was ready to listen to reason. The building had actually belonged to an old friend of Marco's who was doing fifteen to twenty and had signed it over to Marco. Marco told his friend that he had to sell it for a loss. The warehouse had come furnished; at least that's how Marco saw it. An old weather-beaten wooden table with two equally worn out chairs remained in the center of the room. An old bed frame with rusted springs was pushed up against a wall and a brand new mattress rested on top. A lumpy sofa that had seen better days sat crooked in a corner. Old wires dangled from rafters, left over from previous owners. Marco had brought in an old radio to listen to when he wanted to drown out the sounds of the Embarcadero, or Frank, whichever irritated him most at the time.

"You sure it's safe in here?" Albert inquired. His head turned the span of the awkwardly furnished warehouse. Dust, dirt and broken boards lined the floor. This did not make Albert feel comfortable at all. But it was the streams of light coming in from the rusty, stained windows that lent a peaceful glow to its interior.

"Why sure, Albert, just as safe as you are with me." Marco slammed the door shut for effect.

"Now you're going to tell me everything I want to know." Marco walked over to the lone table in the center of the warehouse and pulled out a chair, "Here, take a seat and get comfortable. We may be here a while."

Albert looked down at the beaten wooden chair and its matching counterpart.

"Go ahead, take a seat. I'm not going to ask again."

Albert placed his hands on the splintered table and lowered himself onto the hard seat.

"That's better." Marco took the adjacent chair, turned it around, straddled it and rested his folded arms on the back.

"Shall we get started?"

 ∽

Darcy drove her car as fast as she could without drawing attention. She had a feeling that Mr. Stanton would be on his way to Fulton Street. She figured she had the advantage though, because he would be taking the bus, or so she assumed. Chasing a suspect she admittedly was attracted to, she couldn't help but wonder . . . *what would the other cops think of me?* They already didn't think of her as real cop because she didn't have her "street degree". She had spent most of her time behind a desk learning from books and studying cases. She had agonized during late nights of research and spent many solitary hours going over court proceedings. But the most painful of all was the years of lingering in the background while detectives like Marco charged ahead with exciting and meaningful cases - and glory. She was in the "real world" now and earning that degree - big time. The other cops would surely have to respect her when this was all over, and besides she felt she owed it to her fallen partner to succeed.

Darcy arrived at Fulton Street and parked a block down and across the street from the house which she was sent to watch. Not long after she was settled; a bus pulled up. To avoid being detected she leaned over into the passenger seat and out of sight. The parking brake began to stab into her side. As she heard the bus leave, she rose cautiously in her seat, wincing at the pain. The agony was worth it though, because she was now looking directly at Mr. Stanton heading up the walkway toward the little house. He unexpectedly paused and began to turn around. She immediately directed her attention to the car's console and started the engine. Once she heard the front door shut she turned off the ignition. The scene was clear now, no sign of Mr. Stanton. She continued her surveillance recalling the last time she ran into him. She had actually inserted herself into the investigation, but now she had to remain stealth in her seeking of the truth. She just knew this would lead her somewhere; she just had to remain diligent and watchful. She did have a lead after all, and a good-looking one at that. Darcy smile.

∽

Montgomery's eyes adjusted to the dimly lit room. He took notice of the humming activity in the next chamber and approached.

"Well it's about time." It was Lulu displaying her authoritative disposition, bordering on noxious.

"Hello to you too, Lulu. So how far have we gotten today?"

"Let me have Roger tell you. I can't understand him most of the time," she turned to face Roger who was intensely watching his monitor. "Would you come here, Roger, and explain to Monty just what you're doing in there?" Roger did not look up. His thoughts had drifted back to when he had been working at the Los Alamos National Laboratory in New Mexico. That's when he had been tapped by the Fifth Column. Cloak-and-dagger kind of stuff, but he found it an amusing break from the long hours he put in. He had worked there eight years as a researcher in the development of the quantum computer. Roger had supposed that was the reason they thought him to be a person of interest for their cause. Of course, that was back when the theory of quantum computing was still in its infancy. At that time they had only managed to spread a single cubit across three nuclear spins in each molecule of liquid solution. How exciting *that* had been for him - to harness the power of atoms and molecules to perform memory and processing tasks! And how much more exciting it was a couple of years later to be able to develop a seven cubit quantum computer within a single drop! But that was then. Now the government was holding a big secret close to their vests, but not before he had been privy to it. A twelve cubit system had been confiscated and duplicated. The U.S. could now decode and encode secret information on a much more complex level and at an exponentially more rapid speed.

But that technology was still cumbersome at best, so Roger packed up and went off to UC Santa Barbara to work on a more viable technique. He had told the Fifth Column it would be to all their benefit if he took some more time to study this emerging process and they had agreed. This new technique used diamonds and nitrogen instead of liquids which he found much easier to work with. This was a huge step forward in quantum computers and why Roger now found himself with endless funds to continue to develop the *master* of *all* quantum computers. Since gaining this newfound knowledge and joining the ranks of the Fifth Column, hopefully soon he would become the most valuable person in the technological world.

"Roger, did you hear me?" Lulu had now become emphatically impatient, "did you hear what I said? Hey!"

"Leave the guy alone, Lulu, he's busy," said Montgomery.

"No. These people work for *me* and they're going to show me the proper respect."

"Oh, sorry. You wanted something?" Roger finally returned.

"Yes. I want you to explain to Montgomery what you're doing and how far you've gotten. As a matter of fact, I'd like to know the latter myself."

Roger knew that even if he took all day he could never explain it to them. He decided to try to dumb it down for them and put everything in the simplest of terms.

"Okay. Here is where I work on the quantum computer I built and am continually improving," he waved his hand over his work station like a game show host, "and over here is Marta's computer where she monitors activities at the other end," Roger walked over and rested a hand on the back of her chair. Then pointing to the ceiling he continued, "and upstairs is where we have a dozen OS, or Operating System, computers connected to our network as well as our server which is isolated and locked in what we call our cold room." Roger went back and sat at his unusual looking computer and went on with further explanation. "What *my* computer is doing right now is working on cracking the key, or code, for the encrypted files coming in from NIPPER. This key is probably not very long, meaning the code is probably not that difficult, since these files are all unclassified. Once I have the key then I will convert the cipher text into plaintext."

"What's a nipper?" asked Lulu.

"NIPPER is owned by the U.S. DOD, Department of Defense, and is used by them and the Department of State to transmit information." Montgomery just nodded. "And when the plaintext is complete it will be downloaded onto a computer upstairs."

"Impressive," stated Montgomery approvingly, as if to convey his sympathy for having to work so closely with Lulu.

"Not really. The impressive part will be when I can get through to SIPPER which will allow me access to classified information including Top Secret and SCI from JWICS."

"SCI? JWICS?" asked Lulu, confused again by his use of acronyms.

"Sensitive Compartmented Information from the Joint Worldwide Intelligence Communications System. But I'm waiting on word from Marta to see if she's found a backdoor yet or if we have to create one." Roger looked up to see if they were following him and only caught sight of blank faces. Marta was giggling and Roger shot her a glance. "Marta was unable to use her key logger by transmitting wirelessly. So we then decided to create a worm at the kernel level to install a backdoor in the remote computer. Either way, once we've gained access, their entire network will be under our control. Cool, huh?" Still no response from his listeners. "Well, then next I'll be able to follow the same process as I did for NIPPER on SIPPER." Lulu and Montgomery realized he had concluded his explanation. Lulu still wasn't clear, but knew it sounded good.

"So how much longer until we've got a hold of classified information?" asked Montgomery.

"Hopefully I'll have breached SIPPER in a day or so and begin working on the key. I'm guessing this key will be longer and more difficult to decipher, so it will most likely take a day or two for that as well."

"How soon will we have all the information we need?" Montgomery queried further.

"I'm looking at possibly a week, give or take," answered Roger. Montgomery was amazed at the progress they were making. It wouldn't be long before they possessed sensitive material from the most powerful nation and their allies.

"Alright," said Lulu "sounds good. Do you have my computer ready yet?"

"Yep. Set it up with a one-time pad using symmetric key algorithms so the security will be equal to the length using block ciphers," replied Roger, relishing subtle glee in utterly confusing her.

"*Can I use it?*" Lulu was exasperated; she had no idea what he was talking about, as usual.

"Yes."

"Good. A monosyllabic answer I can understand. I'll let you get back to your work. We have no more time to waste."

ᖰᢩ

Marco sat silently as he waited for an obsequious Albert to begin speaking. But, as usual, he was running out of patience and rethinking the situation. Marco decided it was futile to stall any longer and jumped right in.

"So, Albert, let me begin here. Picture the house on Fulton Street. I can't seem to figure out what's so interesting there. Think you could enlighten me?" Albert slowly raised his head and fixed his eyes on Marco.

"That's where the people in the Fifth Column meet. There are a lot of computers there, the latest equipment and the best that money can buy, pretty nice set-up too. They. . . ." Marco interrupted.

"Wait, wait, wait. Go back to the part where you mentioned some sort of a fifth column."

"It's what they call themselves. Fifth Column. They're a secret group that supports some kind of higher entity. There is one single goal and they will use any means possible to obtain it; even sabotage and espionage. The worst part is that they are quite intolerant of people who make mistakes and of those they suspect may turn on them. You are either *in* or *dead*."

"That seems a little harsh." Marco wondered if this indeed was true or if Albert was just exaggerating. "So let me get this straight. These people are all members of one group working for a single purpose, and if they don't like you they kill you?"

"Yes, that's what I'm saying." Albert looked completely serious. Marco then pulled out his little notebook from his inside pocket and searched his other pockets for a pen. Albert pulled one from his shirt pocket and presented it to Marco.

"Thanks." Marco flipped the pages of his notebook until he reached an unmarked one and continued. "So who's in this Fifth Column?"

"Well, I don't know everyone because we're only allowed to know our direct contacts. But I sometimes hear things that I'm not supposed to, names and such, of people that might be involved." Marco waited for him to name names, but decided not to push, as Albert still seemed a little apprehensive to divulge his secrets. Gentle prodding seemed in order.

"Alright, so what's your role in all this besides murderer?" That was as gentle as Marco could be at the moment. Albert tightened his face at this accusation.

"No, that part shocked me more than anything. That's not what I get paid to do; I'm an accountant for God's sake, not a hit man. I *never* would have killed that guy. I'd go down myself before I'd do that to anyone else." Marco was not yet convinced of Albert's truthfulness.

"So you're an accountant, huh. For what or who?"

"For the Fifth Column mostly. Bradley Ambrose channels money through his newspaper and I make sure purchases are paid for. I pay for all the stuff at the house and the people who run it. The money's always there, don't know where it comes from, it just shows up." *Now we're getting somewhere,* thought Marco.

"So, Bradley comes up with the money. . . ."

Albert interrupted, "No, he just uses bank accounts from the paper. The money comes from Ms. Tremblay. Where she gets it, I don't know. She's the only one who seems to know all the players and all the details of what they're up to."

"Whoa, didn't see that one coming," Marco remarked, astonished at the revelation. "I just figured she was power-hungry, didn't know she was well fed. So that explains her attitude. What a bitch."

"Yeah, well, anyway she seems to call all the shots but sometimes it's hard to tell because Captain Morrison commands everything."

"*Are you kidding me?* Shit! The captain has that much power in all this?" Marco wondered if Darcy was aware of her captain's dealings or if she just might be a part of it herself. Doubts began to eat at Marco. What about Brody? Wasn't that his uncle Morrison was latched on to while bolting out of his office? Is he also mixed up in all this?

A brief silence ensued as Marco processed this latest turn of events. *Crap. Is Brody involved or is he in danger? Crap. Darcy is over on Fulton Street right now . . . is she in harm's way? And Frank, well, crap, I'd better get him the hell out of the hospital, pronto.* Marco realized he needed to be three people in three places all at once but he was stuck here with Albert. He had to make his last questions quick.

"Is there *anything* else you think I need to know?" *Dumb question,* thought Marco, *he's not going to give me anything willingly.*

"Nope. Can't think of anything else."

"Fine then." Marco grabbed up his notebook and tossed the pen back to Albert. He knew he couldn't trust Albert to stay here alone. Marco decided to call on a cop he trusted to watch over him until he got back. Marco picked up his cell phone and dialed.

"Hey, Rick. It's Marco. I need a favor." Marco just listened as Rick gave him a hard time about always needing a favor.

"Yeah, I know, I owe you. Okay, more than one, I get it. But I really need your help. Can you get over to the big orange warehouse on Embarcadero?" Marco listened to Rick's incredulous response. "Yes, now. It's really important. I know I always say that, but this time I mean it . . . it's important." Marco waited through the silence for a response. "Really? That's great! Okay, I'll see you in ten." Marco turned his attention back to Albert.

"I don't need a babysitter, you know." said Albert.

"Okay then, how about a bodyguard? Officer Rick is coming to keep an eye on you while I'm gone. I want you to be real good for him, understand?"

"Yeah, yeah."

"And don't even think of leaving. I'm not done with you. Got it?"

"Sure."

Marco waited for Rick to arrive, made the introductions and rushed out the door, ran to his car and just sat there for a moment collecting his thoughts. *Hospital. Newspaper. Fulton Street. Frank. Brody. Darcy.* Unable to reach Darcy or Brody by cell phone and with Frank unconscious, Marco grabbed his face in his hands in frustration and let out a yell. Suddenly he knew just what to do.

∾

Darcy rolled all the windows down in her car to let the cool sea breeze flow through. It felt refreshing, and she imagined herself on the beach, lapping waves upon the shore, toes buried in the sand, what bliss. Just then Darcy noticed a curtain move in one of the upstairs windows. Did they see her? She didn't think so. Hadn't she parked far enough away? Surely she had. She didn't bother writing it down, she dismissed the incident and went on daydreaming.

∾

Montgomery thought he heard an elephant barreling down the stairs. It was no elephant though; it was a woman and he had to dodge her path as she ran by. She looked vaguely familiar to him.

"Lulu, gotta go. I need to take care of something," the woman informed her.

"Not so fast, Angie, you're supposed to stay here and wait for a call," Lulu ordered.

"I don't think anyone will mind if I eliminate a problem first. This has been a long time coming." Angie didn't care what Lulu said and for that matter the captain. She was determined and understood the consequences should she fail in her attempt. She then liberated a pistol from the cabinet near the front door and tucked it in behind her at the small of her back.

"If the captain calls while I'm gone, tell him I'm taking care of that little problem he mentioned. I'll return soon - and with good news." Instead of leaving through the front door, Angie retreated out the French doors at the back of the house.

∾

Having been dropped back off at the newspaper, Brody went flying through the press room doors and headed straight for his desk. He fumbled with his keys until he was able to grasp the one needed to unlock the desk drawer. He opened it and sighed with relief when he found the now less-mysterious documents were still there. He scrambled to get them into his soft leather briefcase, the one his uncle had given him when he started at the paper months ago. He remembered that was the last time he had a real conversation with his uncle. He was a very busy man, Brody justified to himself regarding his uncle's strange behavior. Brody was so focused on his quest that he didn't even notice when Duncan, having been observing him from across the office, walked past him and out of the office.

Accomplishing his goal, Brody snatched up his briefcase and left just as he came; like the wind. Rushing toward his car he spotted Duncan behind his own car with the trunk open.

"Hey, Brody, come check this out."

"I don't have time, Duncan. I'm in an awful rush. I have a deadline to meet."

"It will only take a second. I can't believe this myself. I've just got to show someone." Brody, not wanting to seem too anxious, relented and headed toward Duncan's car. Just as he leaned in to see what Duncan was going on about, Brody heard a thump on the back of his head and felt a dull pain commence simultaneously. Little white lights began dancing in his vision and then it was dark.

"I knew that kid was trouble, I told them so, but did they listen? No, of course not," Duncan stated to himself aloud as he slammed the trunk shut on the little pipsqueak. He then headed back to the press room, located his desk and sat down. Picking up his phone he dialed an extension and Bradley answered.

"Mr. Ambrose, we have a problem."

❧

Marco rushed into the hospital through the emergency room entrance. He slipped into one of the empty surgical elevators and pressed the button to the fifth floor. Quickly locating a small room he peered inside and found shelves of scrubs and various surgical needs. He grabbed a shirt, pants, mask and cap and ducked into a nearby closet to change. After exchanging clothes he looked around to see what he could do with his previous attire. *Lockers?* No, he didn't plan on coming back. *Trash? Certainly not*, he'd spent a pretty penny on the jeans alone. Then he spied some drawstring bags, snatched one up and made his deposit.

Acting the stealth chameleon, Marco casually strolled to Frank's room toting the bag along with him. An officer was at Frank's bedside wishing him well. Marco was astonished when he heard Frank reply. *He's awake! Good, that will make things much easier.* Marco pulled the mask up over his nose and mouth and went in and dismissed the officer. It took Frank only a moment to realize it was Marco behind the disguise.

"Marco!"

"Shhh. Don't say anything just yet."

"But. . . ."

"I mean it. Do you trust me?"

"With my life, which at the moment seems just that."

"Then do as I say. We can talk when we're out of here. I'm springing you from this joint." Marco lowered the bed until Frank was in a prone position and unlocked the wheels.

"Think you can shut up for ten minutes?"

"I think I can manage that seeing that I'm at your mercy."

"You are. Now close your eyes and be quiet." Marco tossed his bag on top of Frank's legs and pushed the bed down the hall and into the waiting surgical elevator, taking one last look around before the doors closed.

৩০

As Brody entered consciousness he reached around to the back of his head and felt the newly acquired lump. A headache began to take shape and he grimaced at the pain. Opening his eyes, Brody realized he was in the trunk of a car - Duncan's car he now remembered. *What the hell? Duncan, you asshole, this isn't funny.* Brody squirmed, struggled, beat on the trunk and yelled, all to no end. Then he noticed something swinging, glowing in the dark. He was sweating now and finding it harder to breathe. Brody grabbed a hold of the illuminated object and pulled. The trunk popped open and Brody heaved in the fresh air, letting the breeze penetrate his now clammy skin. Not knowing how long he'd been out and how soon Duncan might return, Brody climbed out of the trunk, slammed it down and made a mad dash for his car. *Shit!* He forgot his briefcase. Oh well, he remembered most of what was in his notes anyway. *But what if, no, what will happen when Duncan finds them? Oh well, he probably wouldn't understand the significance of them anyway.* Brody jumped in his car and made tracks to put distance between him and the paper. While making his escape he made a call to Marco. He'd know what to do.

"Hey, Brody. I'm kind of busy right now."

"Me too, Marco. One of the guys at work just locked me in his trunk but I escaped."

"Well good for you."

"No, you don't understand. I don't know what to do now. My notes got locked in there. Everything I've been working on. This isn't funny. I'm serious. This is way out of hand! Can you help me?"

"Wow. Hell of a day, eh Brody? Welcome to my world," Marco chuckled and gave Frank a knowing wink. "Okay buddy, I'll help ya out here. Get yourself to the Embarcadero and find the orange warehouse, it's the only one."

"Okay."

"Go there and wait for me. Oh, and don't be alarmed, Albert's there too along with an officer friend of mine. I've got to go now. See ya." Marco did not wait for a reply and disconnected their conversation. But Brody felt just a little bit safer having spoken to Marco. And Marco felt a little more at ease knowing Brody was safe.

"That's two down, one to go," he instinctively said to his partner, Frank, as if he understood in the slightest what was going on. Frank was too weak to ask and at the moment, just didn't care that much.

༄

Darcy, having finished her daydreaming, began to doodle on her notes when suddenly a familiar face appeared on the driver's side and was holding a gun to her head.

"Angie?"

"I see you still recognize me."

"Of course! But what are you doing?"

"Still bright as ever I see. Well, at the moment I'm holding a gun to your head."

"But why, Angie? You've been missing and I thought you were dead. I've been trying to find out what happened to you."

"All very touching, Darcy, but what's happened is you've stepped in it and now you're gonna have to pay."

"What the hell's going on? What are you going to do?"

Angie just laughed at her, "what I should have done long ago. You got the promotion, you got all the recognition and commendations . . . what did I get? Nothing. That's right . . . nothing."

"You want to kill me over *that*?"

"Oh you simple little girl. Not just that. You are now interfering with my new life. A life where I'm valued, needed and respected. A life with limitless possibilities and plenty of rewards."

"But Angie. . . ." And before she could finish, a car came roaring down the street toward them. Angie only had a moment to realize it was coming for her, but she didn't want to miss her opportunity for sweet revenge. She turned back to Darcy and steadied her gun on her. Darcy reflexively shielded her face with her arms.

Consumed with malicious intent and a tortured frame of mind, Angie underestimated Marco's driving abilities. The speeding car made contact with her removing any doubt of failure. Her body was sent flailing into the air and instantly whisked away from Darcy's sight landing with a pounding thud. Angie lay motionless, the curb now her pillow. Barely conscious she remained consumed with rage. Angie could still feel the cold steel of her gun in her hand but was overwhelmed by the pain that now gripped her body and soul. She struggled to move, not willing to be deterred, but all was in vain. Angie closed her eyes for the very last time, her final thought resting on unfinished business.

Marco came to a sudden halt and reversed the car until he was aligned with Darcy's window.

"Darcy," he yelled over Frank in the passenger seat, "follow me. Now!" Darcy lowered her arms from her face and looked to see Marco and Frank in the car next to her.

"Follow me," Marco implored. And as if having an out-of-body experience, Darcy saw herself engage the engine of her car, slowly put it into gear and follow Marco, never taking notice of her former partner's body now laying in the gutter on Fulton Street.

∞

Brody drove past the warehouse making sure that no one unusual was loitering outside. He parked his car in the parking garage across the street and sat there a moment to ensure he wasn't followed. After exiting his car he opened the trunk, donned his jacket and fixed the collar up high around his neck. He placed his favorite Giants baseball cap on his head and pulled it down tightly. Warily, he crossed the street, treading like a dehydrated panther, until he reached the brightly painted orange warehouse. He looked around cautiously until he felt collected enough to enter. Opening the door he stepped inside and quickly shut it behind him; and in his mind, figuratively closing off the world as he now knew it. As he walked further inside at first glance he appeared to be alone.

"Hello," Brody cried out. No response was forthcoming. *Didn't Marco tell me there would be people here?* Brody's eyes having adjusted to the dimly lit interior walked a few steps further inside. He looked ahead and noticed a wooden chair tipped over on the ground next to a splintered table. Suddenly he heard a low moaning from beyond it.

"Who's there?" inquired Brody, his voice now trembling. "Answer me. I have a gun and I'm not afraid to use it!"

"Don't shoot," a faint voice echoed from across the warehouse, "I'm a police officer."

Brody, believing what the voice had told him, ran over to see what he could do. Observing a uniformed police officer lying on the ground with blood dripping from his face, Brody bent down to help him sit up.

"Wow! Are you okay? What happened?" asked Brody.

"Marco asked me to keep this guy Albert in the warehouse until he got back. I guess Albert had something altogether different in mind. When I wasn't looking, he cold-cocked me and hit me over the head with that chair."

"I'll go get some help," said Brody, momentarily ignoring any danger.

The officer, too dizzy to respond, bent his legs and put his head between his knees. As Brody made a run for the door it flung open.

"Honey, I'm home," it was Marco, "and we've got company."

Brody watched as Marco came through the door supporting Frank under his arm. He then observed Darcy walking slowly and deliberately behind them; she was uncommonly silent.

"Hey, Darcy, were you born in a barn? Shut the door, huh?" Marco bellowed.

Brody noticed she didn't respond to Marco's command and quickly went over, shut the door and locked it as tightly as he could.

"That's right, Brody, lock that door. You never know who may want to huff and puff and blow it down," Marco just laughed. Frank winced as Marco suddenly spun around.

Marco furrowed his brow noticing something was wrong - very wrong.

"Where's Rick? And more importantly, where's Albert?"

Epiphany

"What is it, Duncan? I don't have time for hysterics. I'm quite busy," Bradley did not want to have to deal with any more episodes. His plate was full at the moment.

"But, Mr. Ambrose, it's very important I speak with you right away. Can I come up?"

"No!" Bradley replied insistently, "I've got someone in my office, and I can't be disturbed." With that he hung up on Duncan leaving him to his own determination. Bradley then turned to the edgy guest in his office to see that he was pacing the floor. It was Albert and he had something on his mind and appeared nervously disconcerted.

Without warning, the door to Bradley's office swung open and revealed an outraged Captain Morrison. Bradley stared in conciliation as the Captain abruptly discharged his foot against the door, slammed it shut and headed straight for Albert. "Where have you been?" He growled through his gritted teeth, demanding an explanation.

"I was at the hospital to . . . you know . . . but there were too many cops and they started to notice me. So I had to leave, don't you see?" But no matter the effort, Albert did not appear to be satisfying the captain.

"I'm working with idiots! You had a job to do. What if Frank wakes up and starts talking? What then?" The captain grabbed hold of Albert with a frightening viciousness.

"But Frank's on his way out. He's still unconscious. I'll get another chance. I promise," Albert was now pleading.

"Hah. You think so? Not on my watch - that's for sure. When I give you a job to do it doesn't mean it gets done when you feel like it, it means now!" The captain released his hold on Albert who now stood frozen in the middle of Bradley's office.

"They undoubtedly noticed you skulking about. Why did you take so long? The plan was so simple that even Bradley here could have done it," he made an abrupt motion with his arm toward Bradley, "why should I waste any more time on you?" Bradley remained seated in his chair behind the protection of his desk. He was incredulous over the situation but too fearful to intervene. He watched as the captain strutted in a wide circle around Albert until he was directly behind him.

"I don't believe your story," the captain firmly told Albert.

"It's all true," Albert's voice was shaking now.

"Okay then. Where did you go after you left the hospital?"

"Home."

"Wrong. Try again. Only this time I want the truth from you."

Albert just stood there cognizant of the fact that this was it for him. He was finished here. He tried to do the right thing as he saw it, but, as always, it got away from him. Albert thought that if he came back he would be able to stay in their good graces. What could he have been think-ing? He knew the type of people he was associating with. And it all came down to this - this one single moment. He knew if he told the truth he would put Marco and the others in even greater danger than they already were. Not that he really cared, but if he was going to be taken out of the game, he'd go with all his secrets. Why should he help the Fifth Column now? He completely understood he had run out of chances. He realized he was expendable and with resignation he made his decision.

"Well?" the captain's voice pierced the stillness.

"I went home as I told you."

The next thing Albert felt was the icy coldness of the silencer on the back of his neck. He closed his eyes and sweet death fell upon him. His body dropped to the floor having finally reached a stolid peace.

Bradley was on his feet now leaning with his hands on his desk peer-ing over it, devastated at the horrifying turn of events. The captain disas-sembled the silencer from his gun, took out a cloth and wiped them down, carefully and methodically. He then returned them to their rightful places.

"I'll get someone to clean this up for you." The captain looked up to see Bradley still not moving. He found this somewhat amusing.

"Oh, c'mon Bradley, this can't be the first time you've seen a dead body."

"No, but it's the first time I've seen one get that way."

"You'll get used to it."

"I don't want to."

༄

The group inside the house heard the resounding crash outside.

"What the hell has Angie done now?" Lulu asked with contempt. Montgomery instinctively rushed for the front door.

"Not the front door you idiot. Someone will see you. Go upstairs."

Roger and Marta were out of their respective seats and in the doorway of their room.

"Get back to your desks. No one called for you," Lulu shouted at them. "You have work to finish and there is no time for you to waste standing there gawking. Now go!" The two turned in fear nearly knocking each other over trying to get back to their desks.

Montgomery followed her up the stairs to a room in the front of the house. Looking out the window they could see that bystanders had converged on the scene and traffic began to back up with each honk and shout.

"Oh my God! Is that. . . ." Montgomery was trying to process the scene outside.

"Yep. That's my girl." Lulu folded her arms and shook her head. "Impatient hot-head, serves her right. Now, if you'll excuse me, I have some trash to clean up."

Montgomery watched her callously turn and make her exit. Facing back to the window he saw the neighbors and onlookers were beginning to gather around the body; many with their hands covering their mouths, some holding their hands to their heads, but all seemed sickeningly curious at the sight. And what a sight he thought. Angie had landed in the gutter almost directly in front of the house. He surmised that she did not die instantly, because she seemed to have had enough time to place herself in a fetal position. *Poor girl.* The shouting heard downstairs interrupted Montgomery's thoughts. No doubt Lulu was attempting to call for a "pick up".

Montgomery was half way down the stairs when he saw Winston come through the front door pale and nervous. Neither made mention of the resulting horror out front. It was evident that each of them was well aware. Montgomery didn't have any more time to waste though. He had things to do. He put a hand in his coat pocket, felt the scarf inside, gently squeezed it and smiled.

૦૭

Constance quickly wrapped up her press conference when she saw Captain Dupree heading in the direction of Frank's room.

"Thank you for coming. That's all for now. I'll be back later to brief you on any further developments. Thank you." Constance grabbed her papers and rushed to the captain.

"Captain, wait," she looked at him for a reply or response. "Captain Dupree," she tried louder. He finally stopped and turned toward her. *What now?* He did not want to be bothered right now, especially by her. As he watched her approach he saw her tuck the strands of her auburn hair behind one ear, which now revealed the intensity of her green eyes. He never understood why such a pretty girl would choose to hide behind all that hair. He could, however, understand why she wore those outlandish Bohemian clothes. They completely distracted anyone from noticing her full figure hidden beneath. *Had she always dressed this way? Enough with that*, he thought. He needed to see Frank and she was stalling him.

"What do you want, Constance?"

"Captain, I haven't had the chance to tell you how sorry I am about Frank." The captain just nodded. He did not want to draw out the conversation any more than he had to.

"Have you found out anything more about how Frank got to be here in the first place?"

"That's why I'm heading to his room right now. I hear he's awake. Now if you'll excuse me I'll fill you in later." He reversed his position away from her and continued on to Frank's room.

Constance was not happy with his curt dismissal. She was the spokesperson for the SFPD and liaison to The City, for heaven's sake, and she *had* to stay informed of all its activities, this being the latest among them. She was not going to be put off so easily and decided to follow Captain Dupree.

"Hey. What's going on? Where's Frank? Somebody get in here and tell me where he went!" The captain was shouting up and down the hallway, drawing attention but no assistance.

"What happened?" Constance inquired, as nurses and orderlies began appearing from back offices and patients' rooms.

"Get out of my way! I've got to find out what happened to Frank." The captain was not happy at all with this latest turn of events.

"You'd better find Frank before they do," was all Constance had to say. Feeling she had played a trump card, she turned her back to him just as a crush of doctors and nurses swarmed him directly outside Frank's vacant room. She walked rebelliously out of sight before he could have the opportunity to challenge her comment. Constance left behind a stunned Captain Dupree, now standing in the midst of a bustling hospital ward.

৩৩

Duncan, temporarily alienated by Mr. Ambrose, decided he had better deal with his predicament on his own. He found himself hesitating. *What for?* Because of what that little geek might say? It would be his word against Brody's and who would they believe anyway? Duncan reassured himself that he would come out just fine. He left his desk and made his way through the double doors. Duncan spotted Mr. Ambrose in the building lobby leaving with a police officer. They were walking so briskly that Mr. Ambrose didn't have time to respond to the security guard's polite nod from the lobby desk. *Interesting,* he thought, *but not unusual. Mr. Ambrose is an eccentric old fool after all.*

Duncan continued on to his car. He clicked the button on his keychain and the trunk flew open. Expecting quite something else, he was astonished to find only a lonely briefcase.

"Why that little shit!" Duncan exclaimed to himself. He sat down on the bumper in front of the open trunk to think. Well at least it didn't appear he had gone to his uncle. Not yet anyway. Just then a car sped past, and Duncan looked over in time to see Mr. Ambrose inside. *Hey, maybe my day isn't blown after all.* He slammed the trunk down, jumped into the driver's seat and went off in pursuit of his boss. He was tiring of being kept in the dark.

∾

"Brody, where's Rick and Albert?" asked Marco, clearly annoyed.

"I don't know. I swear. When I got here the place was empty. Well, except for that officer I found lying on the floor over there." Brody pointed to a spot beyond the table. Marco let go of Frank and rushed over to his fallen friend as Brody continued his story. "Then when I realized he was hurt bad and there was no sign of Albert, I thought I'd better get out of here, quick, and get some help, but that's when all of you showed up. Boy, am I glad to see your faces . . . well yours and Darcy's. This must be Frank, nice to meet you," Brody held out his hand to Frank who was clearly not interested in pleasantries.

"Who the hell is this? And why does he not know when to shut up?" Frank winced at another round of pain caused by the strain.

"Oh, this here is Brody. You remember me telling you about him interrupting my peaceful night in North Beach," Marco yelled from beyond the table while tending to Rick.

"Hey!" Brody protested.

"I mean it in the nicest of ways, Brody, really. Now shut up and let me take care of Rick."

Darcy's fog lifted at the sound of the familiar banter.

"Oh this is Marco's sidekick," she jabbed while pointing haplessly at Brody.

"You must be Darcy." Frank strained to look at her. "I'd shake your hand but, well, I'm in a little pain here." He was able to size her up though. *Marco was right she was a knockout. Too bad.*

"Can I get a little help here? Anybody?" pleaded Marco. Brody, in a show of good faith, quickly went to Rick's side to help Marco.

"Let's get him over to the bed and make him comfortable." ordered Marco. The two men assisted Rick to his feet and helped him over to the bedside.

"Thanks," said Rick.

"What happened to Albert?" asked Marco, ignoring his friend's injuries.

"Glad to see you're so concerned . . . about *me*."

"Well I assume you let Albert get the jump on you. That's on you. So how did it happen?"

"Gee, your concern is touching. We struggled and he knocked me out."

"At least he didn't get a hold of your piece, I see."

"Yeah, not like you did with your last perp."

"Ouch. That hurt."

"And so do *I*. Now can you put me down so I can rest? The last thing I want to do is go back and tell my sergeant I've been helping *you*. If he sees me like this, I'll have to say something."

"There are worse fates."

"Not many when it comes to you."

Marco just rolled his eyes and the two men lowered Rick on to the bed and returned to the others.

"So, Frank, what really did happen to you?" Darcy asked.

"Yeah, all I know is what I heard at the paper. They had you tootin' your last horn. Wow. Great to see you made it and all," added Brody.

"Will somebody shut him up? Please?" Frank pleaded as he settled into the hard chair.

Marco shot the sternest of glances at Brody, pointed to the other chair tipped on its end on the dank, dusty floor and put a 'tick-a-lock' over his lips. Marco wanted answers but he was too tired to proceed delicately, so he just decided to be himself.

"What the hell happened to you anyway?" *Maybe I should start over*, Marco reconsidered, "I mean how could you have let this happen to you?" Not much better, but he felt he got his point across.

Through his increasing discomfort Frank managed to say, "I'll answer all your questions if I could please just have a moment to catch my breath."

What is wrong with Marco? Darcy could understand his attitude when Frank was helpless, but Frank was here now - safe. She decided it would be better if she spoke to Frank instead. She walked over to the table nearest Frank, turned around, gently lifted herself up on the surface and sat facing him.

"Frank, I know this is going to be difficult for you to relive what happened to you. But we really need to know," Darcy's voice was reassuring.

"I understand," appreciating her intervention. *Marco was acting so mean, and Brody, well, he was just annoying.* Frank went on to describe the events that landed him in that comfy hospital bed fighting for his life.

"Wow!" Brody was unable to contain himself any longer.

"Shut up, Brody," Darcy shot at him. "Frank, did you get a good look at anyone? Can you describe them?" she inquired.

He continued describing someone familiar and when he finished Darcy stood up and began pacing.

"What?" Marco asked as nicely as he could.

"He just described Angie, my dead, well not dead, but I guess now dead, partner."

"Do you mean she wasn't dead?" Brody was on his feet now too, "but she's dead now? How?"

"Oh, Marco ran her down," Frank stated matter-of-factly, "saved Darcy's life, too."

"What?" Brody looked over at Marco with his mouth hanging open.

"You're welcome." Marco looked over at Darcy who just stared back at him.

"So, I believe we're all up to speed here?" She looked at each one of them.

"Hell no," Brody felt it was his turn now. "Why did Marco run down your ex-partner? I've seen Marco in action - a real cowboy cop. But why would. . . ."

"She must be one of *them*," answered Marco, "she had a gun pointed at Darcy's head!"

"And she mentioned something about working with some people that respected and valued her," said Darcy, "and she sure seemed to hate me."

"Ah . . . yeah! Wasn't that obvious?" Marco sniped.

"Well what about the elevator incident?" Brody pulled out of the air in an obvious attempt to be included, "I was almost killed, well . . . okay maybe injured! I mean, I couldn't breathe and this piece of glass flew and stuck in my leg . . ." he raised his pant leg up to reveal a negligible cut on his shin. ". . . and then. . . ."

82

"No *then*, Brody. You're fine," Marco interjected. "Remember, *I* was the one who was actually *in* the elevator before the damn thing plummeted forty floors!" And he proceeded to tell the tale of his adventure on the fortieth floor.

"You mean Bradley Ambrose *and* Captain Morrison are in on this?" Darcy sat down in the unbalanced chair vacated by Brody.

"Yep. And Albert talked before he disappeared," Marco said. "He gave up Lulu Tremblay, Ambrose's secretary; apparently she's got the goods on everything." Marco waited for the group to process the information and then continued. "They call themselves the Fifth Column; we can probably assume that's who Angie meant she was working for. And I suspect, Winston, the elevator maintenance guy is in on it, but I don't have any proof of that yet."

"Anyone else?" asked Darcy.

"Don't know. I was going to ask Albert but he's MIA at the moment."

"Is that all?" asked Frank.

"Isn't that enough?" Marco teased. "Seriously, though, there is one last thing." He looked over at Brody.

"Do you know anything about any of this? And be honest." They all watched as Brody became introspective, *the little hamster was running on its wheel,* thought Marco.

In a sudden outburst, Brody responded. "No I don't! This is all news to me too! I am hurt that you even asked me that" he shouted to the group. "I bet the guy who locked me in his trunk, Duncan, knows something. Come to think of it, he's been hovering over me like a hawk lately. I didn't pay much attention before, because I've been so wrapped up in this case. Oh no, and now he has all my notes too! Shit. Now they're going to think I'm on to them when I wasn't really, but now I am. Oh, I'm dead." Brody was up pacing again only this time much slower. And while his performance displayed his inherited anxiety, they all knew he was clean.

"I'm sorry, Brody, but I just had to ask. I mean your uncle is involved and we have to be certain who we can trust at this point," said Marco in a rare moment of apology.

"Why don't you just talk to some of your contacts to see if anyone's looking for you before you get too worried?" asked Darcy.

"Ah, about that," Brody hesitated, "I'm, well . . . I really don't have any contacts other than all of you." He closed his eyes and scrunched up his face as Marco advanced nearer to him. But Darcy prevented his approach.

"Brody, what are you trying to say?" asked Darcy.

"Well, one of my tactics is to embellish my position."

"I'll embellish you, you little. . . ." Marco unforgivingly spewed through gritted teeth as Darcy continued to restrain him.

"Let's not worry about that right now, Brody," Darcy invoked, wanting to reign in the conversation and focus on what they needed to do. "What if we come up with another idea then? Let's all discuss this, shall we?"

Darcy felt Marco loosen up and she released her hold on him. She looked thoughtfully at Brody. He wasn't so bad really, as long as she could tolerate his incessant blathering. Then Darcy remembered what Marco had told her the night of Mr. Schultz's demise.

"Marco, remember when you said if we gave Brody details about our discoveries to print it would make some people nervous?"

"I vaguely remember something to that affect," said Marco half-heartedly.

"Well, what if we all put our heads together and let Brody write that article? Write something that tips our hand, just a little, something which may cause the Fifth Column to make a mistake or two." They were all nodding in agreement and a newfound energy seeped into the warehouse.

"We're on the run and outnumbered. There's no better time to turn them upside down and inside out." Darcy felt she had just come up with the best idea ever.

"So who's going to print it?" Brody asked, not sure he wanted to hear the answer.

"Why you are, you twit. And you'll even put your name on it," she emphasized. "We wouldn't want them to misunderstand who's sending them a message."

"Oh boy," sighed Brody.

"You're gonna get the kid killed!" stated Marco, suddenly protective of Brody.

"With three police officers watching him? Why, Marco, what could go wrong?" she teased.

"And we've got time for that?"

"What else are we going to do?"

"Stop the Fifth Column, that's what."

"Baby steps, Marco. We've got the edge. We know who they are now."

"Yes, and they know who *we* are. Big deal."

"The big deal is that *they* don't know that *we* know who *they* are." Marco just threw up his hands in defeat.

"Okay, paperboy, let's get this thing started." She looked over at Brody, "don't worry; you're going to be famous."

"Yeah, a famous dead person," he relented.

❧

With her next press conference being held at city hall, Constance decided to jazz up her ensemble with the new beret she just purchased. She flipped it onto her head and adjusted it down to one side. The mayor was already there and approaching her. Once he reached her side, he embarked on instructions of what to say, what not to say and when to be indirect; she hated election years. It was now nearly time for her to speak. All the media microphones were huddled in place and the reporters were jockeying for the best positions. She advanced to the podium.

"Good afternoon everyone. I'm here to add some details regarding the recent events that have taken place. Our concurrent initial investigations have found no link between any of these cases." She fumbled with her papers. "And now I'd like to present some further information. Detective Frank Belkin was injured while on duty in the Castro District. He was stabilized and released from the hospital. Detective Angela Paxton was previously missing and presumed dead. Her body was discovered earlier today in the Richmond District. The investigation into her death is ongoing. No further details are available." She looked up for a brief pause before continuing. "The two bodies found floating in the bay south of the Golden Gate Bridge have now been identified as Thomas Schultz, a career criminal, and Albert Bouchard, Senior Executive at the San Francisco Bay Daily newspaper." Constance looked up from her notes, "are there any questions?" She took a long breath and prepared herself for the onslaught of inquiries.

"Do you mean to tell us that the department believes these incidences are a coincidence and are in no way related?" There it was - the question she most wanted to evade. Apparently she hadn't made herself clear enough.

"The detectives in charge of each of these cases have gone over them individually and thoroughly. They were unable to find any connection. The fact that the two bodies were found near each other is just a plain and simple coincidence, yes. According to the Coroner's office, the time and manner of death for each victim was quite different, with death occurring at very different times and under very different circumstances."

"So what you're saying is that it was just a coincidence that two of the victims were found at the same time in the same location?"

"That's right."

"Why do you suppose it took so many months for Detective Paxton's body to show up?" *Ah, another gem*, she thought.

"Well, her time of death is recent and we hope with further investigation we can determine the nature of her disappearance and the cause of her death."

"Could she have possibly been kidnapped?"

"Like I stated earlier, the investigation into the whereabouts and death of Detective Paxton require further investigating at this time. I cannot comment any further."

"Ms. Moreau," began the next inquiry. Constance looked down to see that it was her insidious torturer from the local TV station, Martin Jackson. He never missed any of her press conferences and was always ready to poke, prod, needle and embarrass her. She wished she could cut this short, but she had just begun. Martin continued when he realized he had her attention.

"Ms. Moreau, you mentioned that Detective Belkin was injured while on duty. Do you know the circumstances of the incident?"

"Not at this time," she tried not to seethe.

"I didn't think so," he shot at her, but he wasn't finished yet.

"I have tried to locate Detective Belkin for comment but he appears unavailable. Do you by any chance know where he happens to be at this moment?"

"No."

"No? Okay then. Can you please explain the extent of his injuries," Martin smiled slyly at her. It was all she could do not to rip his face off. She took another breath and forced a smile.

"Detective Belkin sustained multiple lacerations and bruises resulting in a concussion and broken ribs."

"Very good. Thank you for that. Now what were the causes of death for the two floating victims?"

"The Coroner's office has not completed their investigation."

"Oh, just when I thought we were getting somewhere. Alright then, *why* does the department believe that none of these incidents are related?"

"Because, Martin, they just aren't," Constance couldn't take it any longer. The mayor sensing the tension, not understanding her change in behavior and not wanting to allow this to continue, stepped in.

"Thank you all for coming. We'll announce another press conference soon. Thank you." And with that he grabbed Constance's arm and led her just inside the front doors of City Hall.

"What the hell's the matter with you? Didn't you listen to a word I said? They told me you were going to be able to handle things out there. What happened?"

"Yeah. Yeah. I heard you. You know, mayor, the world doesn't revolve around you, despite what you may think. I didn't even vote for you and find it difficult to understand how you ever got elected. Now go and do whatever it is a mayor is supposed to do and leave my job to me."

She shoved open both doors, walked back to the podium and snatched her notes. As she was descending the front steps she felt a cold stare upon her. Looking over to the crowd of reporters she saw Martin standing there with that sideways grin of his. Many believed that he'd held up well through his years of experience, but she was inclined to think otherwise. He surely must have been one of the early reporters that had been able to break the color barrier all those years ago. Perhaps that is why he is so relentless. He still believes he's a struggling black man. And besides, his short curly afro was now sprinkled with gray, and he looked a little stockier these days. She smiled back at him.

☙

"Don't rush me. I can't work with all of you just staring at me. Oh, and by the way, not helping me either. So where are all of *your* ideas? You guys are always pushing me, pulling me or brushing me off. But now you need me. Hah! C'mon, you slackers need to work with me here. This was *your* idea, remember? I can't do this by myself," Brody said to them.

"*You're* the reporter here," Frank noted, "or was that just another lie?"

"Of course I am." Brody looked over at Marco for validation. But Marco was distracted by something in his coat pocket.

"Hey, Brody, remember those papers I took from you in your uncle's office?"

"Yeah, why?"

"Well, here they are." Marco proudly bestowed them to the group by placing them on the table. "Let's see what we've got here. Looks like a lot of numbers and names."

"Whoa, these must be Albert's," Brody said after taking a closer look. "He's the accountant over at the newspaper. These look like expenditures for the Fifth Column!"

"Pay dirt!" Marco added.

"Now hold on." Darcy took hold of the pages.

"Spoilsport," Marco directed at her. Darcy just ignored him. She was finding this easier to do.

"Let's see who's on the list first." She began to peruse its contents.

"Well, anyone we know?" Frank was impatient. He was feeling a little better now.

"Let me see," Darcy began, "hmm, oh, here are some we haven't mentioned so far. Constance Moreau. . . ."

"The SFPD spokesperson?" an astonished Frank blurted out.

"Yep. And here's one *I* know but *you* don't, not yet anyway. Montgomery Stanton."

"Who's he?" Marco joined in.

"While I was doing surveillance at the house on Fulton Street, and believing him to be one of our suspects, I saw an opportunity and followed him to a bus stop. We struck up a conversation and ended up seated together on the bus."

"So what happened?" asked Marco.

"Yeah, were you able to find out anything from him?" inquired Frank, anxiously awaiting some pertinent information regarding their case.

"Well, actually, no," replied Darcy, "I ended up having a most interesting conversation with some other passengers. They were talking about a beating inflicted on a cop named Frank and of the elevator breakdown at the paper. I felt at the time I should check to see if any of you were involved or had been injured. I left Mr. Stanton on the bus and headed for the hospital."

"Why did you do that? We're big boys," Marco shot at her.

"I can see that. And you even wear 'big boy pants' too," quipped Darcy. Marco was surprised at her sudden display of sarcasm.

"Good one," Marco returned, "but why did you let him get away? We've tried for weeks to get a hold of one of them and you just let him go? You let this opportunity just slip away? What were you thinking? What kind of detective are you anyway?"

"A very adept one. Anyone else here pass the sergeant's exam?" She paused while the rest of them remained silent.

"No? Then I guess that settles *that*." As soon as she turned her attention back to the papers the others sneered and rolled their eyes.

"Duncan Brewer's on this list," she informed them.

"I knew it. He's scum. He's gotta go down," said Brody doing his best to act tough.

"Calm down. Don't forget our focus here. We have to create a situation where we make these guys nervous enough to lay their cards on the table – face up," Darcy redirected.

"Yeah, and we've got a full deck and a winning hand," Brody proudly stated, feeling he could now keep up with the rest of them.

"That's right," Darcy said and then turned her attention to Rick who had now risen from the unlikely comfort of the old rusty bed. "Feeling any better?"

"Wow, that guy really clocked me," said Rick while rubbing his head, "but I think I should be getting back to the precinct. My shift is almost up," he laughed.

"Don't mention this to anyone," said Marco.

"Sure, I'll just tell everyone I fell into the door of my patrol car."

"No, you idiot. . . ."

"No, *you're* the idiot for believing I'd actually do that and an even *bigger* idiot for getting me into this in the first place."

"Thanks for your help," said Marco sincerely.

"Sure. And don't call me anymore." Rick stood up, snatched his jacket and shot Marco a stern glance as he exited the warehouse.

"Geez. What's up his ass? You try and help a guy out, provide a little excitement, and this is what you get . . . consternation."

Darcy, hoping to break Marco's latest rant, decided to bring him back to the relevance of their situation.

"Hey, Marco, got a radio or TV around here?" Darcy inquired. "I'd like to see what's been going on since we've been focusing all our attention on what to do next. We need to find out if anything's been reported about any of us. We don't want to reveal any information in the article that may enlighten them to what we're actually up to. We just want to get the Fifth Column rattled enough to make a mistake."

"*You're* good," Brody exclaimed, "if you weren't a cop, I'd ask you to join the paper." Marco rolled his eyes again and poked his finger toward his open mouth and gagged.

"I have a radio over in the corner," Marco said, "I think it still works." He walked over, grabbed the radio and plugged it in. He turned it on and they could hear Constance beginning another a press conference. They all leaned in silently to listen.

When it was over, Marco was the first to speak.

"That's my boy! You go Martin! Gotta love it." He noticed the perplexed look on their faces and decided to explain his familiarity. "He was my roommate for a while after college. Great guy. I like him even more *now* after hearing this, and I didn't think that was possible."

"You *know* him? Really?" asked Brody.

"Yep. Haven't seen him lately though. I got busy and he just got married again. You know how it is."

"Do you think he'd be willing to help us?" Darcy asked.

"Is his name on the list?" asked Marco. Darcy looked again.

"Nope."

"Then he's in."

"What about me? What about the article?" Brody asked, feeling the sharp pain of exclusion.

"Don't worry. We still need the article to be written. You'll have your spotlight. But you must understand, Brody, the more ways we can get under these people's skin, the better," Darcy stated.

Frank had nodded off from the strain of it all. Marco raised his arm up to backhand him but Darcy intervened.

"Don't, Marco, Frank needs his rest. The three of us can do this. Now let's get busy, shall we?"

❧

Montgomery had one more thing to do before he left the house, one *very* important task to complete. He reached into his coat pocket, grabbed a hold of the memory stick inside and held it tightly.

Captain Morrison came bursting through the front door with Bradley bounding apprehensively behind him.

"What the hell, Lulu. Can't you control anyone around here? Do I have to do your job for you?" the captain shouted.

"Watch who you're speaking to, Morrison. It is *you* that takes orders from *me*. Remember that." Lulu didn't need aggravation from this pompous ass. "Angie was a liability anyway. She just took care of that problem herself - in a way." The captain started to speak, but Lulu stopped him. "I know. I know. It hits a little close to home, but we're cleaning up now and it should be contained soon."

"Well it better be because we had our own mess to take care of back at Bradley's office."

"I am well aware of what happened. The clean-up crew already told me they had taken care of it." She motioned to the sitting room.

The captain and Bradley walked into the cluttered area and took a seat on the lumpy old sofa and settled in. Winston was just across from them in a battered stuffed chair. Lulu turned on the TV. What they heard being broadcast shocked all of them but one - Montgomery. He had something else on his mind, and was waiting for a suitable time to act. Roger and Marta were once again up from their desks and listening; listening to Constance's press conference from City Hall.

Montgomery took the liberty of their distraction to slip away from view and surreptitiously make his way to Marta's computer. After opening the memory stick he inserted it into the USB port, logged out of Marta's work and accessed the file. After a few keystrokes he began downloading the virus

- one that would create a backdoor without modifying the source code. By sending in his Trojan horse (modifications to the existing key logger program would rewrite the compiler so it recognizes it during compilation) he would open a concealed back door for later entry. Another dubious strength of this virus is that it completely subverts the anti-virus program's disassembler.

Once the file was downloaded, Montgomery removed the stick from the port, deleted his work and slipped out the back door, undetected; emulating the Trojan horse he'd just lodged in their computer.

"Oh my God! Who told her to say all that?" Lulu exclaimed when the press conference had finished.

"I thought you had control of things," the captain's sarcasm was not lost on Lulu.

"Shut up you narcissistic imbecile. It was *I* who told *you* to send a message to those two nosey cops by eliminating Frank. And what of that? *He's still alive*! Now I have two operatives dead! To top it off, we can't find *any* of those cops. Let me thank you for a job well done."

Not wanting to be another target of her rage, Roger and Marta subtly retreated back to their desks.

Outside, Duncan, having pulled up behind the car he was following, decided to crack open the contents of Brody's briefcase. He retrieved it from inside the trunk and sat back down in his car. The more he dug, the more he realized that Brody had done some of his own digging and was actually on to them. Duncan made the decision that Mr. Ambrose needed to be made aware of what his nephew was up to. He shoved the papers back into the briefcase and headed for the door.

గౠ

"What now? Who's at the door?" Lulu was annoyed.

"Winston, answer the door and get rid of whoever it is. Quickly!" she ordered. Winston hurriedly advanced to the door and opened it. He was not given a chance to speak.

"Hey. My name's Duncan and I'm here to see Mr. Ambrose. It's important." Winston looked to Lulu who was already glaring at Bradley. Bradley just shrugged his shoulders.

"Oh just get up old man and go get rid of him," she commanded Bradley, and to the captain, "nice going. You didn't notice anyone following you? You're an idiot."

"You're a shrew and not to mention an abysmal failure."

"Shut up Morrison, you have no idea. . . ." not wanting to waste any more time on him, Lulu turned to Bradley, "go take care of this unwanted intruder, *now!*"

As Bradley went to confront Duncan at the door, Roger came rushing out from his workroom.

"Lulu! Something's wrong! Someone has breached our system!"

"What! How could you let this happen? I thought you told me we were protected."

"We are. But this virus was downloaded here. Marta's computer has signaled us there's a threat attempting to enter our server." Lulu looked over at Marta.

"Hey. It wasn't me. Roger's been with me from the start." Even though Marta was indifferent about taking responsibility; this time she was innocent.

"She's right," agreed Roger, "there's never been an opportune time for either of us to do this much damage, much less had time to think about it. And do you think I'd even allow Marta the chance to destroy what I've built and worked so hard for?"

Lulu realized that this line of arguing was futile and decided to wait to find out who was responsible. She needed the system repaired and running *now*.

"So what's it going to take to fix it?"

"Well, as far as I can tell it appears that someone has got in through the backdoor and downloaded a resident virus."

"I know you must be wondering how the virus got in," began Marta, "while not knowing who did this, we *do* know that since it's a fast infector it was able to piggy-back on the virus scanner, bypassing our anti-virus programs, and will soon infect all the files which have been scanned - which is everything."

"Then how are you going to remove this virus once it takes effect? And how long will it take?" asked Lulu.

"At this point we're still unclear as to how much information we've lost," stated Marta, "it may take us the rest of the day to work on this. We can then find out what we've got left."

"Then do that," said Lulu.

"Well, there is just one more problem," added Roger.

"*Another one?* God save me. What is it?" gritted Lulu.

"When we reboot the server it will temporarily disconnect us from NIPPER's router. This will trigger an automatic signal back to Intelink that we have been accessing their data-base as an unsanctioned user."

"Is there any way around this?" asked Lulu not intending to be defeated.

"Yes, but it will depend on what we find and may take us three to five days to resolve," answered Roger.

"Then do it," Lulu asserted, "get started!" As she turned around she scanned the outer room and furrowed her brow. Something wasn't right, someone was missing.

"Where's Montgomery?"

Resolve

"Okay, I think we're done here," said Darcy, and then turning to Brody, "is that a wrap, paperboy?"

"I really wish you would stop calling me that," whined Brody, "I haven't been a paperboy since I was in college. I mean, yes, I was a paperboy in college, but I also earned a journalism degree."

"No kidding?" quipped Marco.

"Whatever," Brody shot back, "at least I'm working inside now."

"Yeah, and climbing over our backs to move up the ladder," Frank snidely remarked.

"That's enough everyone," Darcy intervened, "this is getting us nowhere again. Now are we all in agreement that this is the article we want to publish?"

"Yeah, sure," said Marco.

"Fine," added Frank.

"I think it's ready," agreed Brody.

"Then let's go paper . . . uh, Brody. We've got to get you to the paper and get our article in print!" exclaimed Darcy.

"Why are *you* going?" asked Brody.

"To keep an eye on *you*, that's what for." Darcy picked up her keys and cell phone, "now let's go. It's getting late and I'm sure there's a deadline for the morning edition. By the way, what time is that anyway?"

"We still have a couple of hours before cutoff. I want to slip the article in at the last minute. That way the editor won't catch it," answered Brody. He began to ponder the many thoughts of how his published article might change his life. *I will finally have my day. People all over San Francisco will see my by-line; they'll know who I am. I'll get the best tables when I go out to eat (which isn't very often), but when it happens, I'll be the one eating right there with the rich and famous. And I'll move to the front of the line wherever I go, be interviewed on TV. . . .*

"Hey, Brody, wipe that shitty-ass grin off your face," laughed Marco "you've got serious work ahead." And turning to Darcy, "you'd better get our star reporter outta here before his head explodes," he continued, quite entertained with himself.

Darcy started to grab Brody's arm but remembered his grievance.

"C'mon Brody. We've got things to do," Darcy said with a jerk of her head toward the door, "I'll drive." Brody snatched up the papers containing their article and followed her out the door.

"Finally," said Frank, "maybe *now* I can have some peace." He painstakingly rose from his chair and Marco watched as he shuffled over to the old rusty bed frame, dropped himself upon the out-of-place new mattress and sighed.

"Ya know, Frank, we can't stay here," said Marco.

"Shut up, Marco." Frank rolled to his back and placed his arm across his eyes and fell asleep.

෨

While enroute to the *San Francisco Bay Daily*, Darcy became lost in her thoughts while Brody was uncommonly stifled; she focused on the nagging feeling that there was something she needed to finish, *but what?* They had completed their article and it was about to be put to bed, *so that isn't it.* And everyone was safe for the moment. Marco and Frank were together at the warehouse and Brody was under her watch, *nothing left to do there.* Then she realized a singular important task she had left undone. Something she started before they all converged on the warehouse. *But I really should stay with Brody while he concludes his errand at the paper.* She looked over at him. He was just staring blankly at the passing scenes as they drove on; his hands tightly clenching the article. With this task nearly completed she did not see the harm in following her instincts. Her decision was made just as they pulled up to the newspaper building.

"You go on up ahead," said Darcy, "put the article in place. I need to go take care of something. I'll come back and pick you up."

"What is it?" asked Brody.

"Never mind. You just go."

"But what if. . . ."

"Get out, Brody."

Brody reluctantly got out of the car, keeping a firm grip on his valued papers and watched as she drove away, leaving him alone; all alone to carry out his important mission. *That's right!* He quickly turned and ran full force through the door and straight up to his cubicle. He still had over an hour to enter the article into his computer and make tracks to get it surreptitiously submitted.

∞

Darcy turned her car onto Fulton Street and continued tortoise-like toward the house. Just beyond the house was the bus stop, and she spotted a tall figure in a very long coat nervously pacing while waiting there. As she slowly approached she recognized the statuesque individual. *No way!* She couldn't be *that* fortunate. But there he was, Montgomery Stanton. Luck was once again on her side. Darcy pulled up alongside the curb next to Montgomery and rolled down her window.

"Hey stranger," and he actually was, she thought, "need a ride?"

"Hey, Darcy," Montgomery returned with adulation, "actually I do. This is very considerate of you." And he quickly got into her car and slumped down in the seat.

"What's that about?" asked Darcy.

"Nothing. I'll tell you later. Now just drive please."

As they drove away, neither of them noticed as a frantic Lulu came charging out of the house, down the walk and stopped at the edge of the driveway. She darted her gaze back and forth and up and down the street, frenzied and furious.

∞

After about an hour of thinking; Marco realized he had come to no con-clusions. He knew then that he could not be completely successful on this case until he knew *why*. Knowing *who* wasn't very much help and neither was *where*. That left him with *what*. *What were they up to?* His brain hurt now, and a dull headache began penetrating his thoughts. He walked over to Frank who was in deep repose and smacked him on the arm.

"Hey, Frank. Sleeping Beauty. Time to wake up before the prince lays one on you," Marco grimaced at the thought.

Frank began to stir. He stretched and let out a long groan.

"So where is he, this prince, I'd like to meet him," Frank opened his eyes and looked over at Marco, "you certainly can't mean *you*."

"Of course not!" Marco stated emphatically, "but we've got to get out of here, keep moving so our location isn't breached."

"You're just being paranoid. Who'd find us here of all places?"

"They found *you* didn't they? Want another taste? Perhaps you liked it?"

Frank scrunched up his face at the thought of another round of pain.

"No? I didn't think so," said Marco as he pulled out his cell phone.

"Who are you calling?"

"My cousin, Sara. She lives over on Balboa and Twenty-Seventh. We can all stay there for a while. No one knows about her. She's always traversing the world and writing. Her books talk of adventure and danger; wonder how she'd actually like to get a taste of what it's really like."

"You read?"

"Shut up, Frank. I'm not the inane drone you think I am. In fact I find her writing very clever."

"You're not going to tell her about all this, are you?"

"Of course not everything; but she *is* going to wonder why all these people suddenly need to stay at her flat. She's going to need some sort of an explanation, wouldn't you? Now get up while I make my call."

While Marco was on the phone, Frank tried, unsuccessfully, several times to push through the pain and get up. When Marco was through with his call, he looked over at Frank. How pathetic he looked.

"What are you waiting for, Frank, an invitation?"

"Can't you see I'm in pain here?"

Marco went over and assisted Frank to his feet.

"Think you can get to the car or do I have to carry you?"

"Sweep me off my feet, my prince," Frank joked as he batted his eyelashes adoringly at Marco.

"Okay, you can turn your burners down now, I get it," Marco said and he turned for the door.

"Hey, how are Brody and Darcy supposed to know where we've gone?" asked Frank.

"Good point. I nearly forgot. Let me give Brody a shout and he can tell Darcy." Marco took out his cell phone and dialed once again.

"Hey, Marco," Brody replied.

"There's been a change in plans," said Marco.

"I'll say."

"How do *you* know?"

"Because I've been standing out in front of the newspaper for half an hour waiting for Darcy, that's how."

"What?"

"Yeah. There's no sign of her."

"Where is she?"

"I don't know. She just dropped me off here and left."

"Did she happen to mention where she was going?"

"No, she just said, and I quote, 'I have to go check something out', end quote."

"Crap."

"Do you know what she meant then?"

"I think I do. She should know better than to go off alone at a time like this. Crap."

"Well, what do you want me to do? Keep standing out here like a sitting duck?"

"No, it's not safe."

"Do ya think?"

"Wait there but move around the corner out of sight and we'll come and pick you up." Marco hung up and dialed his phone again.

"What's happening?" inquired Frank, confused.

"Darcy's gone off on her own. Got a wild hair up her ass and thinks she's a solo act now, that's what." Marco listened to the phone ring at the other end until it went to voicemail.

"Darcy, where the hell are you? This isn't funny. Call me back. Change of plans. We're no longer at the warehouse. Frank's worried." And he hung up.

"*I'm* worried? Yeah, right."

"Shut up," said Marco, "let's go." And with an infrequent act of caring, Marco helped Frank to the car. *Next step, rescue Brody.* Marco hoped this wouldn't become a habit - any of it.

❦

"Mr. Ambrose," began Duncan, "I have something I think you'll want to see." He opened the briefcase just wide enough for Bradley to get a glimpse of the documents inside and said, "They're Brody's notes."

Lulu, returning from outside, heard this and remained close.

"So? What have they got to do with me?" asked Bradley

"Everything," Duncan replied.

"Get inside and shut the door," Lulu commanded Duncan, "you're being conspicuous." She pushed Bradley to one side, yanked Duncan through the door, took one more look outside and closed it behind her. She turned to the two men and her piercing eyes translated calculations like the humming processors in the next room.

"Now what's this all about?"

Duncan, fearing repercussions held the papers out to her.

"What's this?" Lulu's voice tightened.

"Uh," was all Duncan could manage.

"Uh is not an answer," Lulu was used to getting what she wanted and she wanted and explanation *now*. "What are those papers?"

"They're Brody's notes," Duncan managed to say.

"And?"

"Well," he decided to just jump on in, "Brody knows more than we think he does which means he most likely told those cops."

"What does he know? That little worm can't possibly hurt us," Lulu stated confidently.

A brief yet eternal silence slipped into the room.

"He knows about the Fifth Column," Duncan blurted out.

"No way," said Bradley, "the kid isn't *that* good."

"Oh, but he *is*," said Duncan, "he even knows that we're here."

"What?" Lulu screamed, causing Duncan to step away from her.

"And he got a hold of Albert's expenditure report with everyone's name on it," said Duncan, retreating further back.

"Oh no," said Bradley.

"'Oh no' is right," said a seething Lulu, "he's got to be dealt with - *and those cops too!*"

"We can't just go around getting rid of everyone. There has to be another way," reasoned Bradley.

"Okay, little man, what's *your* strategy?"

"Misinformation. Something that would lead them in a completely different direction."

"Oh, real good, you really think that will work? Look how far they've gotten already with so little. No. I say we remove them from the canvas. What we're working on is too big, and we don't have the time to play games."

Captain Morrison felt that now was a good time to speak up.

"That does seem a little impulsive, Lulu, but I'd expect nothing less from an impetuous fool such as yourself," said the captain.

"Why you. . . ." Lulu could not find the words.

"What's that?" asked Morrison, as she just stood there livid at his remarks. "Here's what *I* think," and he put an arm on Bradley's shoulder, "why doesn't Bradley here reel in Brody?" Turning to Duncan, "and Duncan, how about *you* go and find Brody for us, huh? Don't touch him or even confront him, just find him." Morrison then looked over at Winston who was trying to remain unnoticeable. "Winston, do you think you could manage to track down those nosey cops for us? They can't be too hard to find since Brody's notes seem to indicate they've already been sniffing around here."

"Wait a minute you puffed up buffoon," Lulu started toward Morrison who just held up his hand at her advancement.

"Look who's found her voice," he laughed.

"I've found more than that, you ape. You can't just start giving out orders around here. That's *my* job!"

"Well if your job is bringing more attention to the Fifth Column, then you've been completely successful. I'll give you that. Duncan, Winston, get going and report back to me." He looked at Duncan, and then at Winston. Neither of them had even made an attempt to move. The balance of power teetered.

"Go on! NOW!" Morrison shouted at them.

Lulu stood there and waited, glaring at each man. Duncan, having decided the captain was much bigger than she, tucked the notes under one arm, the briefcase under the other and rapidly scurried out the door. Winston, recognizing the serious shift, decided it would be best if he took the captain's order and followed suit. Morrison turned to Bradley, who was now clutching his chest.

"What now, Bradley?" asked Morrison.

"I don't feel so well."

"Let me take you home and you can rest then."

"Oh that would be good. And you send Brody to me. I'll straighten him out. You'll see." The captain secretly had no intention of doing that. In fact he completely agreed with Lulu, just not her obvious tactics.

"Alright then, let's go old friend." And the two men left for Bradley's house in the Marina, leaving Lulu alone.

"Oh no you don't, Morrison," she said aloud to herself, "this isn't over." Her mind was still processing, yet each tactical lead that flashed before her seemed to be consumed by evasive black holes – like a virus. Lulu made her way to Roger and Marta who were intensely working on resolving the virus issue.

"I'm leaving you two alone now," she began, "I trust that you will continue with what has to be done." There was no response. They were too lost in their work - and this time she didn't mind them not responding. They were carrying out *her* orders. At least she hadn't lost control of the most important part of the mission; the data retrieval. She wasn't about to relinquish it either, especially not to the likes of that ignorant oaf, Morrison. Lulu grabbed her bag and headed for home.

⁊

Constance decided to go to her office to rework some of her notes for an upcoming press conference. At least she'd have the office to herself this time of night, without all the civil servant idlers breaking her concentration.

Unable to locate Frank, Captain Dupree had become anxious and fearful of what might have become of him. Having run out of options, he decided to go to see if Constance might still be in her office. Her foreboding comment, 'find him before they do' was weighing heavy on him, chipping further toward unease.

Dupree pulled around behind the city building and entered through the rear door. After having made entrance, he turned and took the stairs, finding himself slowing the farther he ascended. It became evident to him that he had let himself get completely out of shape. When he reached the door to Constance's office he found it open and she was on the phone speaking. He stopped to listen out of view – and to catch his breath.

"No, Lulu. It's just that I let that reporter get to me," she paused as Lulu was obviously having her say. "Of course I won't let it happen again." Constance spun around in her chair to face her desk once more and began rapping her pen steadily on top of it. "I know you told me what to say. I tried to handle it myself." She bit her tongue; she didn't need to piss off Lulu, especially with all the recent "incidents". "No, I understand. Next time I'll do just what you tell me." She now bit her lip. "The mayor? No, he's an idiot. He's too interested in himself to notice anything else." Constance hoped this interrogation would end soon. "Okay. Okay. Alright. I'll see you then," and she hung up and flung herself back into her chair flopping like a rag doll, finally relieved the conversation had ended. Looking at all the papers on her desk, she realized she could no longer concentrate. Rising from her seat she grabbed her briefcase and shoved them in making ready to leave.

Captain Dupree wasn't sure what to make of the conversation he just heard. His heart had caught up to him, but his mind was far behind. He decided he needed to think this through a little more before confronting Constance. Dupree slipped away from the door and hurried back down the stairs and got back into his car. He did not notice his actions had been observed. He waited only a moment, turned on the engine and headed for Coast Highway.

Dupree always did his best thinking while driving on this winding stretch of road and then stopping to watch the fierce whitecaps turn into gentle waves upon the sand. Even in the darkness, as tonight, the full moon shone brightly on the ever turning crests. The sound of the surge upon the surf and the smell of the salty sea air always cleared his mind. He began to think about how he hadn't had much time lately to ponder his pending retirement. He was too worried about Frank. *And where the hell is Marco? Why was he running around with Sergeant Barlowe? Whatever the reason, it can't be good.*

As Captain Dupree reached Coast Highway and was just settling into a tranquil resolve he noticed a car behind him moving closer at increasing speed. He lazily stuck his arm out the window and waved for the car to go around him. He wasn't going to be pushed into speeding. He wasn't going to take any chances on this road – he knew it too well. Looking in his rearview mirror, Dupree saw that the car had backed off.

As his vehicle traversed a change in decreasing grade and approached a treacherous curve, all that protected the motorist from a gaping cliff perched above the ocean breakers fifty feet below was a lonely guard rail. Suddenly Dupree was blinded by the reflection of light emanating from his rearview mirror. He reached to switch the mirror's angle when he was forcefully hit from behind on the passenger side. The steering wheel took on a mind of its own and spun swiftly out of the control of his left hand. His right hand was drawn down by the force and caused him to lean on it, bracing for leverage. With all his strength Dupree tried to gain control of the steering wheel as the car continued spinning across the lanes. Then, with a sudden jolt, the rear of the car came to rest against the guardrail. Dupree was breathing heavily now as he realized that the motion had stopped. With little light to see by, he leaned out to check his position. As he felt the chill of the ocean air, he was momentarily calmed.

Without warning, the other car returned. Its light, coming from the front this time, blinded Dupree. He frantically clutched at his seatbelt to try to extricate himself. He dared not look away from the approaching vehicle. Had he not always been able to stare danger in the face and survive? The car made impact and the guard rail gave way like the snap of a pencil. Dupree relived all of his accomplishments until the reflection of the moon materialized off the crumpled front of the car resting at the bottom of the cliff.

The other vehicle reversed its position and sped away. Captain Morrison just smiled. He didn't usually like getting his own hands dirty but felt Dupree deserved the honor of captain to captain. *This certainly will send the strongest of messages to those hack detectives*, he decided. Besides that, he was able to pull it off covertly, unlike a certain hateful shrew he was stuck working with. He took a long, deep breath of the moist sea air and decided some music was in order. He pushed the knob on the tuner and smooth jazz resonated from the speakers. "Music to soothe the savage beast," he said aloud, laughing. Morrison then continued home. A weariness was creeping up on him and he wanted to be rested for when he would knock Lulu off her self-made pedestal. She was just too unstable for his liking.

∾

Brody was waiting on the corner behind the *San Francisco Bay Daily* for Marco to come and pick him up when he suddenly realized that, in his haste, he'd left his computer open to the file which contained his article. He immediately did an about-face and raced back inside the building. Once at his desk he was relieved to see no one around. Just as he pressed the delete button, he felt a presence behind him.

"Hello, Brody," said Duncan, "I didn't think you were *that* dedicated to be found here this late."

"Yeah, well what are *you* doing here? By the way, you know there are laws against stalking, and for that matter locking people in trunks of cars!"

"Oh, well that, I was just joking around."

"Well it wasn't funny and I know what you're up to."

"Really? And what's that?"

"I really shouldn't say 'cause we're all alone here. And frankly I don't trust you."

"Is that so? Well I happen to know that your uncle is in his office," he lied, "let's go and have a talk with him. He'll straighten everything out."

Brody thought for a moment. That would be two against one, two for the Fifth Column and one for the good guys. But his uncle was family and surely that would count for something.

"Okay, Duncan, let's go," said Brody calling his bluff.

Duncan wasn't sure why Brody chose not to resist, but he wasn't going to question his good fortune. It will surely make it easier for him to restrain the little peckerhead.

The two rode the elevator absent of any conversation. Brody was busy running scenarios in his mind. *If anything did happen then Marco would surely come to find me when he doesn't see me waiting at the corner.* Brody let out a sigh of relief.

The elevator doors opened on the fortieth floor. From across the room Bradley's office could be seen but the lights were out and it was dark; an impending doom permeated Brody's consciousness. Duncan led the way through the outer doors toward the inner office. The elevator doors slammed shut behind them. It was too late to run now.

"Well look at that. Dark. I was sure Mr. Ambrose hadn't left yet. He must certainly still be working," said Duncan, "let's go see."

Brody, not wanting to be trapped in a room where there was only one way out, looked around the outer room for an excuse not to go in. The door to the storage room was left slightly ajar and a light was streaming from inside.

"Hey, isn't that door supposed to be locked? Doesn't my uncle keep confidential stuff in there? I'm gonna have a look inside."

Brody went over to the door and stepped inside, just a little. Duncan saw his chance, but was also curious as to what secrets were hidden inside. Brody stepped in a little further when he saw Duncan was not following.

"Wow," Brody feigned excitement. "Look at this! Hey, Duncan, come here, see for yourself," beckoned Brody, using the same ruse Duncan used on him before being clobbered and stuffed in his trunk. Brody could only pray that using the same obvious ploy would work on Duncan's little pea brain.

Duncan eventually walked inside and shuffled past Brody to have a closer look for himself. *Why not?* There was plenty of time to do what he had to, and besides, maybe he could find something that would give him an upper hand.

Once Duncan was far enough inside, Brody slowly backed up past the door, slammed it shut and locked it.

"How do you like that, Duncan? Huh? Of course it's much roomier than a *trunk*!"

Brody then went to make sure his hunch was right. Stepping into his uncle's office he saw no sign of him. But upon closer inspection he realized the office was very different from when he was last there. *When was it?*

Probably six months or so he guessed. He noticed several monitors and a console that weren't there before. Brody walked over to investigate. He looked around the console to find a way to turn it on. He spied a green button. *It can't be that simple.* He pressed it anyway. The monitors came to life and he was surprised by what he saw. Each monitor was split into four sections and captured views from all over the building, even the elevators. *Why would my uncle need all this surveillance?* The pounding on the closet door broke his concentration. Duncan was yelling something inaudible. Brody warmed and relished himself with a quiet chuckle.

As he relaxed into a proud moment, Brody suddenly remembered that Marco was on his way to pick him up. He quickly left the console, stopping only for a moment outside the closet door to gloat over what he had just accomplished.

"Have a good night, Duncan."

Once downstairs, Brody rushed out the door and ran directly into Marco.

"I thought you said you'd be waiting for us," Marco said, "Frank was worried."

"I wish you'd stop saying that," Frank yelled out the car window.

"I was, but. . . ."

"Tell me in the car. Let's go."

While they drove, Brody told the tale of his recent exploit.

"So Duncan's locked in a closet?" asked Marco.

"Yep. Serves him right too for locking me in his trunk."

"Bet you're feeling real good about yourself right now," Frank interjected.

"Well, I sort of do, but I feel a little sorry for Duncan too."

"Never feel sorry for the bad guys," warned Marco, "they'd do the same or worse to you."

"Yeah, just look at me," Frank managed to say with a painful grimace.

"Oh," Brody commented and fell silent, but only for a moment. "Hey, where are we going anyway?"

"To my cousin's flat," Marco informed him.

"How much longer?" asked Brody, "'cause I really gotta use the can."

"Oh my God!" Frank blurted out, now exasperated. Then looking to Marco, "do we really. . . ."

"Yes," returned Marco.

⚮

Marco decided to cruise past the house on Fulton Street on his way to Sara's to see if his suspicion about Darcy could be confirmed.

"Hey, isn't that the. . . ." Frank tried to say.

"Yes," Marco intentionally interrupted before Brody could discover where they were. And as he scanned each side of the street he did not see any sign of Darcy or her car. *Crap.*

"What are you looking for?" asked Brody, quite confused.

"Not now, Brody, we've got to keep moving," replied Marco. Then he turned the car on to Twenty-Fifth and swung on to Balboa. Driving slowly toward his cousin's he caught a glimpse of the Golden Gate Bridge to his right. He never tired of the sight of her majestic stance. Before he knew it he was at Twenty-Seventh. He looked up to see that the lights were on in Sara's flat. Marco found an open space and parked.

"We have arrived," Marco announced.

"This doesn't look so bad," observed Brody, "I was expecting something like another one of your dismally furnished warehouses; knowing you. Which I would surmise you find quite adequate."

"No, Brody, Sara's the successful one in the family. She has a yacht at the Marina too. I've often planned to take someone special there one day, you know - pretend it's mine."

"You never took *me* there," joked Frank.

"That's because *you're* not my type," returned Marco. They exited the car and Marco walked around to the trunk, opened it and pulled out a large overstuffed duffle bag.

"What's that for?" asked Brody.

"Extra clothes and stuff for just such an occasion."

"What about us? We can't keep running around in the same stale outfits."

"Outfits?" laughed Frank, "where are you from?"

"Alright, *clothes.* Satisfied?" returned Brody, "I mean we've been in that dirty warehouse and I sweat bullets in a trunk. My clothes are now quite ripe. Would it be possible to run by my place and let me get some clean clothes?"

"No," said Marco, "you two can borrow some of my clothes. Besides, they'd probably look better on you than the ones you seem to pick out for yourselves," he laughed. "Now let's go." He led them up the stairs to the entrance of Sara's building and rang the bell. Marco straightened his hair and turned to Frank and Brody.

"I want you two to be on your best behavior. Sara's very special to me," said Marco.

"Are you *sure* she's your cousin?" asked Brody with a smile as if he'd discovered a dark family secret.

"Listen, Brody, I'm not kidding. Act out of line and I'll throw you out on the street with my bare hands," said Marco, "and yes, she really *is* my cousin."

As the door opened a sensual beauty was revealed to the men. Sara's short wavy auburn hair fell suggestively over one eye as she tilted her head to one side. She leaned invitingly on the open door, looked up and locked her green eyes on her cousin.

"Marco!" she exclaimed, "what a nice surprise. And you brought friends, too. How cheery." She relinquished her hold on the door, "come here and give me some sugar." Sara embraced Marco, clenching tightly. It wasn't until she stepped back that Brody was able to make more than a casual observance. She had the most kissable lips he'd ever seen and her provocative choice in clothing was jaw-droppingly revealing. He decided he'd like *his* body pressed up against her voluptuousness as well. He stepped toward Sara, but Marco held out his arm to prevent his advancement.

"I tried to call you to let you know we were coming, but I got your voicemail instead," Marco informed her.

"You should have left me a message, silly," teased Sara, "but it's not like I would have listened to it anyway. I checked my messages on my way home, well at least to see how many there were. Too many, I decided, so I didn't bother to listen to any of them. Does that make me bad?"

"Not at all, Sara," said Marco, smiling, "oh, and these are my. . ." he paused, "this is my partner, Frank and this is Brody, he works for the *San Francisco Bay Daily*." Brody was disheartened at such a detached introduction, but he smiled anyway. Sara smiled back.

"Well come on in, guys," Sara motioned them to enter, "the place is a wreck. I just got back yesterday from Africa and didn't have a chance to straighten up," she began moving things on the coffee table, "that's not entirely true. I just didn't feel like it, that's all."

Marco caught Brody ogling her as she was bending over and back-handed him across the chest so hard it nearly knocked the wind out of him. Brody grabbed his chest, looked up and noticed the many posters hanging on the walls of her flat. They were book covers. Brody's favorite books were there. Marco was glad to see he was able to avert his attention.

"Hey, Sara," said Brody, "you like these books too? *African Eye, Leg of Luxor, Dally in Durbin, Edinburgh Ear. . . .*" his voice trailed off as he heard Sara laughing.

"What's so funny?" asked Brody, "*African Eye* is my very favorite book. You must like it too or you wouldn't have it and all these other book covers hanging so large on your wall."

"I do, Brody," she responded, "I *wrote* them." And Sara and Marco looked at each other with a smile.

"You?" asked Brody in amazement, "then that's how you can afford a yacht."

"Ah, Marco, you told," said Sara playfully.

"It just slipped out," confessed Marco, "it won't happen again. I promise."

"Too late," she said. "Now we have to take her out on the bay tomorrow."

"Really?" asked Brody.

"No," Marco firmly protested, "we've got some things to take care of before we can waste time cruising on the bay."

"Oh, Marco," said Sara, "you're such a buzz-kill."

"Well, actually I'm trying *not* to get killed," said Marco.

"You've always been so dramatic. You're just like one of the characters in my book, *Edinburgh Ear*," she winked at the others.

"If it's who I'm thinking of, no way. That guy was so gay," he turned to Frank, "no offense."

"None taken," Frank dazedly replied. He was too weary to wave his rainbow flag right now. He walked over to Sara's overstuffed red sofa and helped himself to its billowy fluff. Reclining to a prone position he shoved a pillow under his head and soon all conversation had ceased, at least as far as he was concerned.

"Well I see Frank's found a place to settle," said Sara, "I can put you two in my guest room for the night."

"I was going to talk to you about that." Marco displayed his duffle bag.

"What now, Marco? Who are you hiding from this time?"

"Well, we're not exactly hiding, it's just that a very important case has come up and we all need a place to lay low for a while."

"Thanks for the notice. It's a good thing I had my maid prepare the flat while I was away."

"Sorry about that. We just . . . well things are moving so quickly, the case is really fluid at the moment, and we just don't know where it will take us."

"Are you going to let me in on it? Maybe give me some fodder for a new book?" asked Sara.

"Well, I can't tell you everything, at least not yet, but we can talk in the morning if that's alright with you." Marco yawned, "And Brody here is really beat and needs his beauty sleep." Brody was about to object but caught himself. He now realized this was Marco's MO. Sara was thinking the same.

"C'mon you two," said Sara, "I'll get you set up in the guest room."

They followed her down the narrow hallway to the first room on the right. Looking inside they felt as if they had just landed in the African savannah.

"Like it?" she asked, "I was inspired."

This was more than inspiration, thought Marco; this was her very own African wildlife preserve. There were colorful, carved wooden masks and animal heads which dotted the walls, jutting out precariously. A zebra skin rug partially covered the hardwood floor and the curtains really weren't curtains so much as they were straw and beads dangling over the window. In the center of the room was what looked to be a canopy of some sort draped loosely over the bed. Large white sheer curtains covered the top, cascaded to the floor and encircled the bed. A lantern on the side bed table warmly lit the room and revealed African themed books and magazines on the shelf below.

"See? Just like Africa," Sara stated proudly. Marco managed a smile and turned toward Brody.

"Brody, you go settle in. I just remembered I have a call to make."

"Who are you calling now?" asked Brody.

"Rudeness," quipped Sara.

"Sorry," began Marco, "but this is really important. I've gotta call Martin."

"Really?" Sara asked excitedly.

"You can calm down. He just got married again."

"And he didn't wait for me? The bum."

Marco rolled his eyes at her and then walked down the hallway to make his call.

"Well, I guess it's just you and me, kid," said Sara smiling.

Really? Me? The possibilities raced through Brody's mind. Noticing the look of anticipation on his face, Sara realized she'd reached the end of her game. She tussled the hair on top of Brody's head, turned and crossed the hall to her room.

"Good night, Brody," and she closed the door to her boudoir. *Tease,* thought Brody, and he went and took a very cold shower.

꙳

Montgomery directed Darcy to the Presidio and chose a solitary locale to park the car. She found herself facing the Golden Gate Bridge in the near distance. The nightly fog was just settling atop the very tip of the expanse. Montgomery rolled down his window and Darcy did the same only leaving her hand to rest upon the door's handle. The distant gentle waves could be heard crashing on the rocks below. The moon was newly full and cast a subtle serene blanket of light around them. Darcy admitted to herself that she was more than a little apprehensive. *What have I gotten myself into now?* No one knew where she was, and that was her fault. She was on her own and would have to rely purely on her instincts on this one.

"Well, Darcy," Montgomery broke the silence, "I suppose you're wondering what we're doing all the way out here. All alone," his voice was ominous.

"A little," said Darcy, her quivering voice betraying her.

"I'm here to let you in on a little secret, and then we'll take care of business."

Darcy suddenly realized that she'd put her gun in the glove box. She shot a glance over at it.

"That won't be necessary," said Montgomery as if reading her mind, "We're just here to talk. Is there anything you'd like to say before I begin?"

"No," was all she could manage because there wasn't any *one* thing she wanted to say. There were too many questions. She couldn't choose. They all just circled in her mind.

"Alright then, let me begin," Montgomery took a breath, "Some of what I tell you, you will find hard to believe. And most of what I say you will think is completely incredible. But perhaps the most remarkable thing I will tell you is that I'm working for the U.S. government assisting in putting a stop to the Fifth Column."

Darcy was prepared for just about anything he could have said except for that. *How did I miss this?* Well at least her tenacity paid off and has put him in just the right place to help her new alliance accomplish . . . what? She was sure it was only a matter of time and he would explain it all to her. *What a coup!* He could be the key to their success, or the other way around. Whichever it was, it was good she thought. A wave of comfort enveloped her and she found it reassuring.

"You mean you're on *our* side?" Darcy laughed nervously, releasing any remaining tension between them.

"Do you find that amusing?" He asked. "Is it so difficult to believe?"

"No, no. It's just that I thought you were going to kill me."

"Did I frighten you?"

"A little."

"Tell the truth."

"Okay, you frightened me."

"Good. That was my intention."

"Why?"

"Because it's obvious you're alone and unprepared."

"Unprepared?" asked Darcy incredulous at his accusation, and uselessly defensive. Montgomery pointed to the glove box.

"Oh, that," she said, "You caught me."

"That's right," said Montgomery, "I win." *Damn*, she thought. She ended up being the mouse.

⟳

"How's it going, Marta?" asked Roger, "We're almost out of time. They've just about caught up to our location." He became increasing worried as the signal he was bouncing off worldwide proxy servers was losing ground.

"Nearly there," she returned, "okay, worm ready. Put it in and shut the door!"

Roger hurriedly pounced on his keyboard, madly pushed the keys, loaded the worm and locked the back door.

"That was close," he said while wiping the sweat from his face with his sleeve.

"Sure was," said Marta as she rapidly entered the code to upload the files. "I'm going to upload again. I'm isolating any data we captured from NIPPER. Once I've retrieved the files I will download them onto a computer that I've disconnected from our network. Then we can check later and see if there's anything salvageable."

"Great. That was quicker than I thought."

"Yeah, I guess it helps to have people chasing you."

"And someone on your ass!"

They both laughed until they fell back in their respective chairs, exhausted.

"How about we take a break?" asked Marta, "we've been at this for how long now?"

"About nine hours . . . *straight*."

"Yep, then time for me to check out," she said while taking leave of her chair, "you take first watch. I'm going upstairs and get at least a few hours' sleep."

"Okay," said Roger, now rubbing his eyes, "but could you make a strong pot of coffee before you go up? Otherwise I don't think I'll make it."

"Sure," yawned Marta as she stretched and left him to remain monitoring their devices.

"See you in a few hours," he yelled out to her. Roger extended his arms to loosen his muscles and then smacked his face a few times. He pulled up his sleeves and grabbed his water bottle. Seizing a large gulp he felt only mildly energized. "How's that coffee coming?"

～

Having made his call to Martin and expecting him in the morning, Marco trudged his bone-tired body past an unconscious Frank and back to the "wild kingdom". He was spent and exhausted and just wanted to get a few hours' sleep before heading out again. He'd forgotten all about Brody. Marco walked over to the bed and pulled back the hanging sheers to reveal an unwanted bed partner.

"Hey!" exclaimed an irritated Marco, "get your ass out of my bed! NOW!"

"What?" asked Brody from a slumbering haze.

"Get up!"

"No. I'm tired."

"So am I. I'm tired of you always getting in the way; tired of the way you always have to make a novel out of every conversation; tired of you always being so much trouble. Now move!" Marco then lunged on the bed and with full force pushed Brody onto the floor. He threw the comforter and a pillow in a heap on top of him.

"That's better," said Marco and he flopped his weary body onto the mattress, closed his eyes and sleep fell hard upon him. He didn't care that he'd just hurt Brody's feelings. Or maybe he just didn't understand that Brody looked up to him. But the hero had fallen, fallen hard and so had Brody, literally. Brody scooped up the comforter, gave the pillow a few good whacks, put his head to rest upon it and was off to a world where he could be the hero of his dreams.

～

Darcy was still trying to process the fact that Montgomery was one of the "good guys", and he silently let her do so.

"Wow," she began, "that's something else." She turned to face him bending her knee and tucking her foot under her other leg. Grabbing hold of her hooked appendage she was now ready to ask, and have answered, the many questions Montgomery knew she was going to throw at him.

"I have some questions."

"I bet you do."

"How about we start with the Fifth Column. We seem to know who they are; at least we think so, most of them anyway. But what we don't seem to understand is what they're doing and why," she was serious and back on her game now.

"The Fifth Column," said Montgomery leaning back in his seat and allowing its curves to mold to his body; then looking out the front window, "is a group of very dangerous people."

"I've gathered that."

"Perhaps, but not just because of what you may already know. They don't seem to understand how to work together; they don't play well with others, so to speak. There also seems to be a power struggle going on from within their organization. But besides that, everyone seems to have their own agenda. Sure they all appear to be working on one mission but each one of them has a personal reason for doing so and expects a personal outcome. That is their weakness and that will be their downfall."

"Can we play to their weaknesses?"

"Sure we can."

"Then, tell me, what is their mission?"

"Manipulation of world power."

"That seems grandiose."

"Possibly, but you'd be surprised at how close they've come."

"How?"

"They have these two computer geniuses, experts in each of their fields. Roger has managed to build himself some sort of quantum computer which can break codes and encrypted files at lightning speed."

"I thought quantum computers were science fiction and still in the developmental stages."

"They are, but somehow Roger has managed to create one."

"What files are they after?"

"They are breaking into Intelink."

"What's that?"

"It's a group of secure intranets used by the U.S. intelligence community, including the DOD. There are many classifications streaming data across it. The one they've managed to breach is NIPPER, which, for them, was just a test because it only contains unclassified data. When I left they were just about to breach SIPPER, which contains classified data. That would include Top Secret; SCI, which is Sensitive Compartmentalized Data; and JWICS, the Joint Worldwide Intelligence Communications System."

"No way!" exclaimed Darcy, "you mean *that's* what we've stumbled on to? No wonder they've come at us with such fierce brutality."

"That's not all. After that, they plan on hacking into an Intelink which is run by the CIA. That will be their link directly to the White House."

"Wow! I can just imagine the power they'd have. And I can't even conceive what the repercussions might be?"

"That's why I'm here. But my cover's blown now.

"How?"

"I infected their network with a virus - a strong, fast-moving one. That may set them back a day or two, but I was trying to buy some time by delaying their progress until I could put them out of business for good. I also installed a Trojan horse I can access later remotely."

"How do they know it was you?"

"I don't think they know yet, but I was the only one who had the opportunity."

"Well, Montgomery," Darcy held out her hand, "welcome to the light of day and our gutsy little band of champions." They shook on it.

ာ

After several hours cozied in a dead sleep, Marco sat bolt upright in the bed. Actually, he was dreaming that he *was* dead and Brody was talking non-stop between sobs at his motionless body. *Crap, even in my afterlife I can't escape him*, he lamented. And there had been Frank, wiping gently falling tears from Darcy's eyes. Darcy! Had she called? Marco looked at his cell phone, no messages. *Crap. What's happened to her? Why hasn't she called?* He dialed again and this time it went directly to voicemail. Her phone was turned off. This raised a more intense uneasiness inside him. He was frustrated that he could only leave another message; one he hoped would be returned soon.

"Darcy, this is Marco. Call me back as soon as you get this message. It's important."

Now Marco was restless. He got up and checked the door. Locked. Checked Frank. Sleeping. Looked in on Sara. Asleep. Looked over at Brody. Out. He pushed through the hanging sheers, crawled on top of the bed, rolled to his back and sighed. Putting his hands behind his head he decided to examine the situation. But sleep had another idea.

༄

"Since we seem to be coming clean," began Darcy, "I might as well tell you that my last name is not Baker but Barlowe."

"I know."

"Show off."

"And I know all about your rag-tag group of lionhearted men and have studied each of their dossiers. Even *yours*, Darcy Barlowe."

"Really? So you went J. Edgar Hoover on us, huh? But alas, we know very little about you. Does that seem fair?"

"I'm not that interesting a fellow. I have a job to do and I'm working at it."

"Too vague. What job?"

"To take down the Fifth Column."

"All by yourself?"

"Not exactly. I've got the U.S. government behind me. I work for a covert branch of DHS, Department of Homeland Security. I was only supposed to infiltrate and report on the Fifth Column's activities. But when I saw how much progress they were making, I decided to act instead."

"Well that was either very daring or very reckless of you."

"Probably both. Now I'm not only going to have the Fifth Column after me but my agency as well. I'm supposed to check in every six hours and it's well past that now."

"Call them."

"I'd rather not."

"Then I'll call and see how the boys are doing."

She was able to focus her vision more clearly now that the sun was rising, presenting a welcome light. Reaching for her cell phone she found it was dead. She plugged in the charger and the phone came to life. She had two messages from Marco but decided to forgo listening to them and call him directly. She reasoned that he couldn't be *that* worried; after all he left only two voicemails.

"Marco, its Darcy," she began, "yes I know, I. . . ." she decided to let him go on with his rant. "I'm fine, really," she inserted, but Marco persisted. Before long Darcy detected a pause; she used the opportunity to assert herself back into the conversation. "Okay, so where are you then?" She listened carefully as he gave a description of their new location. "I know where that is. Alright, we'll be right over." He questioned the 'we'. "I'll explain it to you when I get there. I've got some answers for you that will blow you away. On my way now, see ya." Darcy was through tolerating Marco's temper tantrums. She looked over at Montgomery who was looking back sympathetically.

"This is it. Are you ready?" asked Darcy.

"As I'll ever be."

Crescendo

Having exhausted all leads in his search for the elusive cops, Winston determined it would be a good bet that at least one of them would show up at the house on Fulton Street. He pulled up a few houses down and waited. His patience would be tried for sure, but he was banking on Brody's notes. Looking around at how quiet the street had become, he nervously laughed at the thought of failure. It was the failure of others that caused this calm. And it was also due to Lulu and Morrison's erratic behavior. He shuddered at the notion that he'd better be correct in his assumption that the cops would show up here. He just *had* to be successful in locating them . . . or someone, be it Lulu or Morrison, would have his head - literally. Winston had grown tired of all their impulsiveness, but he knew he could never leave; after all, he knew the rules.

❧

Duncan, decidedly having time on his hands, began to investigate the contents of the storage room which held him prisoner. He rummaged through some files and found nothing remarkable. He tossed them all on the floor. Noticing some unmarked boxes behind the files, he grabbed each one and tore them open. Nothing. Then he spotted a large metal box secluded in the corner. He tried not to get his hopes up. Duncan pulled the box from its hiding place and tried to open it. Locked. *Of course it is*, he thought. He looked around for something to pry it open. He crawled around on the floor; perhaps someone dropped something, anything that could be of use. Nothing.

As he was rising up from the floor he saw a set of keys hanging, hidden under a shelf. Duncan snatched them up and tried each one in the lock on the box. At long last one of them worked and he threw open the lid. He was ecstatic with what it was he saw. There were several passports. Each was of a different nationality, but all of them contained Lulu's photo under different names. And he found bankbooks, lots of them, containing balances of not thousands but millions of dollars! Underneath these were some overseas communications and a list of contacts. *Pay dirt!* Having pulled out all the papers, Duncan carefully spread everything out on the floor. Taking a last look inside the box to make sure he hadn't missed anything, he was startled to find a gun. He left it where it was. He had never handled a gun and wasn't about to start.

Now, thought Duncan, *what to do with all this stuff?* He couldn't just take it. So, he decided instead to make use of the only technology he had available to him, the camera on his phone. That way he would have some leverage for later - just in case he needed it. And with these people he knew he was sure he would.

Duncan painstakingly arranged each piece of documentation and photographed it. *Brody was right,* he surmised, *there really was something of value hidden in here.* Once he was finished photographing, he meticulously placed all the materials back in the box and locked it. He pushed the box back into its hiding place and straightened up the mess he'd created. He put all the boxes and files back into place and tucked his phone safely into his pocket. With nothing left to do, he put his ear to the door to listen if anyone had shown up yet. Receiving only silence, Duncan figured he might as well get some rest. He turned off the light, sprawled on the floor and smiled at his successful maneuver. *Boy, Brody really was a putz.*

෧๛

Leaving the Presidio behind, Darcy drove on toward The City. The buildings cast their shadows, leading them as the sun continued to rise. The air was commonly cool and seemed to refresh the senses of both Darcy and Montgomery.

"I can't wait to tell the guys about this," began Darcy, "we've been beating our heads against a wall and getting nowhere."

"Well I'm glad you approve."

"*Approve?* I'm elated! Looks like we'll have the upper hand for a change."

"It's conceivable, but we'll have to remain organized in our methods," warned Montgomery, "or we'll suffer the same fate of the Fifth Column, exposed to weakness."

"*That* I understand. I've been wrangling the boys for a while now. It will be good to have some help for a change."

"I'm glad you see it that way."

"Of course, this clinches the deal, partner."

Just then Montgomery noticed she had turned onto Fulton Street. "What are you doing?" he asked, "didn't you listen to anything I told you? What if they see me?"

"Are you frightened?"

"No."

"Tell the truth."

"Oh, I get it. Payback. You've had your fun. Now let's get out of here!"

As they drove off, neither of them noticed that they had picked up a tail and someone was now trailing them.

∽

Brody emerged from an uncomfortable sleep. As he stretched, a twinge set upon his back and led him to jerk in sudden pain. Hitting the nightstand he precipitated all the books and magazines to plunge onto his head. Protectively he raised his arms and rolled over to a safer position. Now wide-awake, the memories from the night before slipped back into his mind; Sara mocking him and Marco snapping at him. *Why does he even bother?* He decided right then that he was going to be a "new and improved" Brody. He would become cold, callous and heartless. No longer the butt of *anyone's* jokes. He would be just like them.

Brody picked himself up off the floor and pushed open the sheers hanging from the bed. No sign of Marco. Noticing the chill had not only permeated his soul but his body as well, he realized he would need more than just his jockeys to keep warm. Locating the duffel bag, he dug deep inside until he found just the right combination. A pair of jeans, white t-shirt and a short-sleeved, button-down, blue plaid shirt. Brody found the jeans to be a little loose, even with the t-shirt tucked in, so he used his belt to cinch up the waist. He put on the plaid shirt and decided to leave it open. *There! Done.* Once dressed, he realized he was hungry. The smell of coffee and bacon had reached the room. In his rush to head to the kitchen, he slipped on the zebra-skin rug and plummeted to the floor with a resounding thud. He heard laughter emanating down the hallway, and an uncommon rage welled up from within him. Brody regained his balance and his composure. Straightening his clothes he caught a glimpse of himself in the mirrored, closet doors and liked what he saw. He was feeling more like Marco by the minute.

"Shhh, he's coming," Sara softly said. "Now let's be nice, okay?"

Brody walked purposefully down the hallway, across the living room and turned into the kitchen nook to address them. But before he could speak, Frank chimed in.

"Hey, Marco," Frank slapped Marco's arm, "he looks just like *you*." The two men snickered.

Sara walked over and put her arm around Brody. "Don't listen to them. They don't care like I do."

"Whatever," said Brody and he grabbed her arm and flung it off him. He walked over to an empty chair and sat down. "What's there to eat?"

"Well someone got up on the wrong side of the bed this morning," said Sara.

"I slept on the floor," Brody snarled.

"Oh, then that explains it. Would you like some coffee, darlin'?"

"Yes," said Brody trying his best to be demanding, "and with cream."

"Right away Sir Grumps-a-Lot," returned Sara as she went off to get him his coffee.

Marco slugged Brody in the arm, "what the hell's the matter with you?"

"Don't hit me," said Brody coolly in return.

"Whoa, Marco, you'd better watch out," Frank sarcastically warned, unable to contain his laughter.

"I mean it, Brody, stop it!" said Marco through his gritted teeth.

"What?" asked Brody, feigning ignorance. "Why don't you just leave me alone?"

"Uh-oh, one of you had better back off," chuckled Frank, "or at least take it outside."

But before any further offence could be hurled, Sara showed up with Brody's coffee.

"Here's your coffee, Mr. Brody sir," Sara facetiously offered. "I hope you find a better attitude inside that cup." She looked over at Marco, "what's wrong with you?"

"Nothing a little fist-fight wouldn't cure," seethed Marco.

"Oh, now, tuck away your testosterone, boys," Sara admonished, "I want to have a pleasant breakfast with my cousin and my new friends. Anyone want pancakes?"

"I would." Brody smiled as he sipped his coffee.

Lulu, feeling somewhat more refreshed, arrived at her desk but found no sign of Mr. Ambrose. She thought it odd that the only source of light in his otherwise darkened office was the illuminated console and all its monitors. She cautiously went inside, looked around and found no one there. *Idiots.* As if it wasn't bad enough the outer office door was left unlocked, but this? This was just downright irresponsible. She was going to have a talk with Bradley about this. After shutting down the console she went to her desk and sat down. Picking up the phone she dialed Bradley at home.

"Bradley, why are you still at home?" Lulu listened to his excuse. "Oh, you've taken ill. Well you still have some things you need to take care of," she remained attentive but tired of his never-ending illnesses. "Uh-huh, oh I see. Well I'm sure Duncan will find Brody," she rolled her eyes, *the inept following the inept.* "No, no. You get yourself over to the house. Uh-huh, sure, take your medication," *oh this just keeps getting better,* she thought.

"What? You don't think you can make it?" now she was pissed. "Okay. Then I'll send Morrison over to check on you. Okay. Bye now." She slammed the phone in place. *Maybe the old goat will just croak and save her the trouble.* Bradley was getting to be just too much.

Lulu decided that since Bradley wasn't coming in and Morrison was who-knows-where, she could be more effective over at the house right now. She was feeling mostly confident, but still had the perception that she needed to be looking over her shoulder. So, just in case, she determined it would be best to take her locked box along with her. *It's probably not safe to leave it here any longer*, she thought, especially since she found the office fully exposed. Taking her keys in hand she walked over to the utility closet, unlocked it, opened the door and turned on the light only to find Duncan sleeping on the floor inside.

"Duncan!" she yelled, "what the hell are you doing in here?"

Awakening to Lulu's shrieking, on instinct he jumped up to face her. "Stupid Brody locked me in here."

"Stupid *you* for allowing him to do so."

"I know, I know." He hung his head in embarrassing disgrace.

Lulu looked around inside to see if everything was still in order. Duncan noticed her momentarily scrutinize the corner where the metal box was hidden. He shuddered at how close he'd come. Good thing he straightened up the place.

"Go sit over on the sofa," she commanded.

"But. . . ."

"Did you hear me?"

Duncan did not respond but followed her order. Lulu moved some boxes until she reached the locked metal one. *Still locked. Good.* She shot a glance to where the key was kept and found it still there. *Good.* Everything looked to be in its place, but she still didn't trust Duncan. He was too shifty for her liking.

"Duncan," she yelled, "get in here and help me."

Duncan moved quickly across the reception area and into the closet. Lulu pointed to the metal box.

"Take this downstairs for me and put it in your trunk. You're taking me to the house."

"But. . . ."

"What's wrong with you? I know I'm speaking English." She reached down and grabbed the keys from under the shelf. "Come on. Let's go."

Duncan hoisted the box up into his arms and hurried out of the closet. This wasn't the freedom he had pictured all those long hours trapped inside. Lulu slammed the closet door and locked it. Duncan was already waiting at the elevator for her.

"Good boy," she said, "now that's more like it."

৩৩

"Well now who can that be knocking on my front door?" asked Sara, lacking sincerity. She opened the door to reveal Martin. Marco was already on his feet heading for the door.

"Hi, Sara," said Martin, not sure how he would be received.

"Why you rascal. You never called me back, and Marco tells me you're married again. You ol' heartbreaker."

"Well, Sara, you're a tough one to catch. You're like a butterfly, and I just don't have the right net."

"Still the sweet-talker, I see."

"Hey, Martin," Marco interrupted, "good to see ya. Come on in."

"I could hardly sleep after you phoned last night. So you've got an exclusive for me, right?"

Having heard this, Brody felt an impending doom for his rights to their story.

"Wait just a minute," began Brody and he looked to Marco, "You said *I* was getting the scoop on writing your . . . our story. What gives?"

"Calm down, Brody. No one wants steal your glory. . . ."

"Glory? You think *that's* why I'm doing this? Why I became a reporter? Then you don't really know me, do you? I thought by now you would have figured out that I'm worth more than the words I put on paper, that maybe I had become your friend. Boy was I wrong. Maybe I should just leave."

"Brody, you know it's not safe for you out there. And besides, we *do* need you. I'm not going back on my promise. Martin is just here to provide another avenue to help put the pressure on the Fifth Column," said Marco trying his best to calm Brody.

"That's all? You haven't changed your mind?"

"Not at all," assured Marco, "now let me get Martin up to speed. Have another cup of coffee and try not to interrupt . . . it's very annoying."

Not completely satisfied with Marco's take on things, and still a little confused, Brody took his advice anyway and headed for the kitchen.

"Okay, Martin, why don't you come over here to the sofa and we'll talk." The two men walked over to the plush accommodation and sat down. Just then, there was a pounding at the door.

"What now?" Marco growled while unholstering his gun, "Frank, get that."

Frank drew his weapon while Brody, Sara and Martin withdrew to the hallway and held their breaths. Marco aimed toward the door while Frank, from behind the door, opened it. In flew Darcy and an unfamiliar man.

"Geez," said Darcy, "I didn't know I was going to the O.K. Corral." Frank shut the door behind them and holstered his gun. Marco lowered his weapon.

"Now it's a party," Sara interjected as she approached the new arrivals, "you must be Darcy, but I'm sure I don't know this fine looking gentleman." She then turned to Martin, "you can be jealous now."

"Alright. Alright. Enough," said Marco, "let's all get acquainted, beginning with *him*," Marco raised his gun and pointed it at Montgomery.

"That's not very hospitable, Marco," said Sara.

"We'll see," returned Marco, "now who are you?"

"I'm the Fifth Column's worse nightmare," said Montgomery. Marco cocked his gun, not appreciating the response.

"Tell him, Montgomery," pleaded Darcy, "or he may accidentally shoot you."

"I *never* do anything accidentally," said Marco, "now talk."

"Well, it is a little intimidating having a gun pointed at one's face," Montgomery began calmly. Marco raised his gun higher.

"Just tell him," said Darcy.

"My name is Montgomery Stanton and I work for the U.S. government; actually a covert branch of DHS, the Department of Homeland Security. My efforts are to put an end to the Fifth Column." Marco did not move.

"And you believe him, Darcy?" asked Marco.

"Yes," she said, "he's got information for us too. Information we can use against the Fifth Column."

"But isn't this the same guy you were following?"

"Yes, but he was undercover there. Now his cover's been blown and he needs our help."

"So," said Marco, "what's in it for us?"

"The upper hand," said Darcy.

And that was all Marco needed to hear. He liked the idea getting the jump on these people for a change. This losing streak was wearing thin. He lowered his gun and holstered it while the others let out a collective sigh of relief. Marco held out his hand.

"I'm Detective Marco Morelli," he said, and pointing out the others, "this is my partner, Detective Frank Belkin, over there is Brody Abernathy from the *San Francisco Bay Daily*, my cousin, Sara Hall, this is her flat," and putting an arm around Martin, "this is my old friend, Martin Jackson."

"Yes," said Montgomery, "I recognize you from the news. Great job, by the way."

Now that the introductions were over, the room fell silent except for the bacon heard sizzling in the background.

"Well," said Montgomery, "looks like you have all your bases covered where the press is concerned." He paused to inhale the aroma, "is that breakfast I smell? I'm famished. Do you mind if I partake in some sustenance?" He flirtatiously smiled at Sara.

"Why not at all," Sara returned coquettishly, having fallen prey to his disarming charm. "You just come right over here and sit down. What would you like? How about some coffee first?"

"That would be delightful," replied Montgomery.

"Oh, aren't you just the refined one," said Sara. She turned to the other men, "and the rest of you should take note."

Unbelievable, thought Darcy, *he's just like every other man, especially around a pretty woman.*

∾

Captain Morrison arrived at the West End precinct to find chatter reverberating throughout the office. No doubt they'd heard the shocking news of Captain Dupree's death. Attempting to make a beeline to his office, he was sidelined by a group of detectives.

"Captain, have you heard?"

"It's just horrible."

"Captain Dupree is dead."

"His car fell off a cliff on Coast Highway."

"Really?" feigned Captain Morrison, trying his best at sincerity.

"Yeah, and the worst part was it looks like he must have survived for hours waiting for help."

"Who found him?" asked Morrison, beginning to worry.

"We're not sure yet."

"We've got Ratchet and Meyers out looking for witnesses. So far they've come up empty." *Good*, thought Morrison.

"Alright, get as many detectives and officers you can spare on this one," commanded the captain, "I'll be in my office. No doubt fielding calls from the mayor and the city council." He continued toward his office. The closer he got, the more irritated he became with the continuing blather from the detectives spewing suggestions and suspicions regarding Dupree's death. When he reached the door to his office he could stand it no more and he turned to address them.

"Well," he shouted, "what are you waiting for? Do I have to tell you what has to be done?" The room fell silent. "Call the Special Unit and see where you can be of assistance. That's an order!"

The captain slammed the door. He walked over to his desk, sat down and smiled. *That's how it's done, Lulu*, he thought to himself. Morrison reached over, picked up his phone and dialed Lulu's cell phone.

"Lulu, where are you?" asked the captain. She explained she was on her way to the house. "Why aren't you at work?" He listened, her voice grated on him like sandpaper. "What? Bradley's still at home feeling ill? What a waste of time he's become." Morrison became even more annoyed. "You agree with me? That's gotta be a first. Yes, yes. I know. Dupree? No, I didn't have anything to do with that," he lied, waiting to see if she agreed. "No." Lulu went on with her diatribe and he just sat there and took it, any disagreement now would tip his hand. "Yes, I do see that it works out well for us." He paused to let her give one of her tiresome orders. "Sure, I can get away. I have a few things to take care of first, as you might expect. Yes,

I know it's important. I'll be there as soon as I can." And he hung up on her, giving him only moderate satisfaction.

∽

After finishing their breakfast, Sara cleared the table while the others retired to the living room.

"Don't start without me," hollered Sara, "I don't want to miss anything."

Marco decided to begin with something that had been nagging him. He turned to Montgomery.

"So, who's pulling Lulu's strings? My gut tells me there's a lot more to this than just her."

"You have no idea," said Darcy, "tell him, tell them."

"Well, the first thing I'm sure you'd like to know is what they're up to," Montgomery proceeded, and they all nodded in agreement.

"Tell us. We want to know everything. What are these pathetic psycho maniacs up to? Do they know about us? I hope not, but they probably do. What can we do now?"

"You can shut up, Brody," said Marco, "let him speak."

"Okay," returned Brody, "but I just want to make sure he tells us all of it."

"I'm sure he will," said Marco, and turning to Montgomery, "won't you?"

Montgomery then went on to explain everything to them, not leaving out a single detail. There it was. Everything he knew out on the table.

"See," said Darcy, "I told you he could help."

"You weren't kidding," said Marco, "except you didn't explain exactly who is in charge of the Fifth Column."

"We are most certain that it's someone or a group of people overseas," began Montgomery, "because Lulu has been communicating via email somewhere out of the country. But the address and files are encrypted. We have someone at the NSA, the National Security Agency, working on them now, but it's slow going. At this juncture we won't be able to cut the head off the snake, but we can deter it from its latest prey, Intelink."

"If DHS and NSA are involved then I think Captain Dupree should be aware of this," said Frank.

"Can you trust him?" asked Montgomery.

"With my life."

"Then why don't you go ahead and secure his support. He may have access to resources not available to us at the moment."

"Sure, I'll just go home and change and then head over to his office."

"Hey," said Brody, "how come he gets to go home and change and I can't?"

"I swear, Brody," said Marco, "quit whining, complaining and interrupting!"

"Oh, I see. Now that the article is done and I risked my life to get it into print, I'm relegated to a bothersome whiner?"

"*You* said it, I didn't."

"You know, this mission, or whatever it is we're on isn't finished yet, and you still need me to wrap it up in the paper. The readers have only gotten a taste of what's to come."

"Wow, what a bloated sense of self you have. I will concede that we need you here, if only to keep you safe. Now put things back into their proper perspective, like a good little reporter, and remember you are here to *observe* not *participate*. Got it?"

"See what I mean?" asked Darcy of Montgomery, "your turn to wrangle."

"Okay everyone," began Montgomery, "let's all think here for a minute." He turned to Frank, "you go on ahead to Captain Dupree's office; good idea you had there." And wanting to split up Brody and Marco, "Marco, why don't you and Martin head over to the house on Fulton Street and see if you can spot any activity or persons?"

"Great," said Martin, "let's go, Marco. We can take my Jag."

"When did you get a Jag?" asked Sara, "you must be doing very well."

"Never mind," said Marco, "Okay, Martin, let's go." He turned to Darcy, "and make sure your cell phone is *on* this time."

The three men, Frank, Marco and Martin, left the flat. Brody was waiting for his assignment.

"What should I do?" asked Brody.

"Stay here with us," commanded Montgomery, "you're much safer here." He turned to Sara, "do you happen to have a computer?"

"What kind of a question is that to a writer?" asked Sara mockingly, "of course I do."

"Oh, sorry, I didn't know."

"Here's a hint," and she fanned her arm around the walls, "these are all my books."

"Impressive," said Montgomery, but needing to get down to business, "would I be able to make use of your computer for a bit? I need to try and disable the computers over at the house on Fulton Street."

"Wow. You can do that?" asked Brody.

"Yes, it may take a while and we're running out of time. Sara, would you please show me to your computer?"

Sara walked over to a roll-top desk that was pushed up against a wall in the living room, rolled up the top and turned. "*Voila.*"

๑๏

Captain Morrison, feeling he had spent enough time in his office to appear concerned, decided to head out to the house. He exited his office and found it gratifying to notice the absence of idle chitchat. They all appeared to be busying themselves with one thing or another. *Good.* He was able to make his escape barring any further conversation, got in his car and headed to his real job.

๑๏

Having reached their destination on Fulton Street, Marco instructed Martin to park a few houses down.

"Now what do we do?" asked Martin.

"Wait."

"Mind if I turn on news radio? I need to get my fix."

"Knock yourself out."

Shortly after the radio was turned on, a breaking news report was announced. Martin turned up the volume.

"And early this morning a car was found plunged off a cliff on Coast Highway," came the reporter's voice, *"The body of Captain Vincent Dupree was found strapped in the vehicle."* Marco grabbed hold of the dashboard, *"It appears he lost control of his vehicle, slid across lanes and through the guardrail. At this time it is being considered an accident. Further details will be announced later at a press conference at City Hall."* Marco turned off the radio and remained silent.

"Isn't that your captain, the one Frank mentioned he was going to see?" Martin inquired of his old friend.

"Unfortunately you're right on that one, Martin. Dupree and I may not have always gotten along or seen eye-to-eye, but bottom line, he always had my back."

"I'm sorry, Marco."

"Nothing to be sorry about," said Marco, his anger intensifying, "it's *them*, they did this to him and now they've crossed the line. First Frank and now Dupree. They're not going to get away with this."

"You mean the Fifth Column did this? But they said it was an accident."

"And *you* believe that? That's just what they want us to think. You know better than that, Martin."

"Well, what do you want to do now?"

"First let me call Frank. Then we'll go over to the precinct so you can report on the truth before they clean this up with more lies at the press conference."

"Will do. Let me call my cameraman first so he can meet me there."

"You can do that enroute. Let's go now while we still have the jump on them."

"Copy that," said Martin. And as he sped off toward Marco's precinct, neither of them noticed the oncoming car with Duncan and Lulu inside.

Marco grabbed his cell phone and dialed Frank.

❦

"Just park across the street," Lulu instructed Duncan as they arrived at the house, "and bring that box inside for me."

Duncan parked the car and extricated the box from his trunk, which seemed to be seeing a lot of action lately. Just as they were making their way across the street, Captain Morrison pulled up. He was annoyed to see Duncan.

"Lulu, what's he doing here?" asked Morrison, "and what's in that box?"

"I invited him," said Lulu, "and the box is none of your business."

How odd, thought Morrison, *she invited a minion?* And there must be something in that box; he was going to make it his business to find out just what it was. He stopped to pick up the newspaper that had been delivered. While Lulu and Duncan entered the house, he unrolled the paper and exposed the front page. All at once his face turned red, his mouth fell open and he stopped breathing. He could hardly believe the startling headline; and worse was the fact it was written by Brody Abernathy. Morrison shoved the paper under his arm and rushed inside to read it.

Dangerous Secrets in San Francisco

By Brody Abernathy

You may have been wondering why no clear answers have been forthcoming to explain the recent surge in criminal activity in The City; and why the SFPD is keeping San Francisco's citizens in the dark. I have decided to reveal what I know; which at this point, I realize, leaves more questions than answers.

There are people in very high places in this city committing very sinister acts. As a result, they have chosen to annihilate anyone who gets in their way. These people have formed an illicit coterie; an illegal, exclusive group of people who are unified by one menacing purpose that is eminently threatening to our community.

Proof lies within the recent deaths that have captured our headlines. Do not believe it when you are told that these are isolated incidences. Each death was a cold and calculated move on their part.

Detective Angie Paxton, previously presumed dead, betrayed her oath to serve and protect the people of San Francisco and instead became a member of this devious group. She has since been found dead in the Richmond District. Can this be considered proof of vengeance served upon betrayal – betrayal of this band of criminals? It is believed to be the case.

Albert Bouchard, a fellow *SFBD* staff employee, was also a member of this mysterious group. As an accountant, he was able to provide funding - even money laundering for their cause. He was also one of two people (the other was Det. Paxton) tasked to kill Detective Frank Belkin. Did Mr. Bouchard receive the likewise fate of death upon failure? My evidence points to that conclusion.

Thomas Schultz, a low-level, repeat-offending thug was another member of this group. He supplied them with stolen key electrical and technical components. Perhaps he was permanently silenced because his position had been compromised? We may never know because the SFPD has conveniently misplaced any documentation pertaining to his detainment.

It saddens me to say that my uncle, Bradley Ambrose, owner

of this newspaper; and his secretary, Lulu Tremblay, have also been linked to this group and appear to be major players within its hierarchy. My fellow reporter, Duncan Brewer; and maintenance engineer, Winston Gagnon, round out those from the *San Francisco Bay Daily* who work for them.

But the most chilling fact is that, Captain Andrew Morrison from the SFPD West End Division is strategizing, manipulating, delivering and covering up this secret group's murderous activities in an effort to advance the group's eventual goal.

Do not be disheartened by this message. Be assured that there are plans in place to take down this troubling group that has been menacing our city. And, God willing, I will be around to report it to you.

"Lulu," shouted Morrison, "have you seen this?"

"What are you bellowing about this time?" returned Lulu.

"Look at *this*!" He shoved the newspaper at her. Morrison stood there anxiously staring at her while she read the article.

"How did this get printed?" asked Lulu, still processing. She turned and shouted, "Duncan, get in here!"

What now? Duncan wondered.

"Do you know anything about this?" Lulu crammed the newspaper into Duncan's chest. He unrumpled it to reveal Brody's article - right there on the front page! *So this is why the little runt was there last night.* After he finished reading, a thought crossed his mind, *Brody, what have you done?*

"Well? What do you have to say for yourself? Did you know about this?" spit Lulu.

"No. I don't know anything about this. I can't imagine how it got there," replied Duncan.

"Liar!" shouted Lulu, "you were there last night with Brody. Why he even locked you in my closet! You had no idea what he was up to?"

"None."

"You're worthless," Lulu repulsed. She grabbed the newspaper from him and tore it to shreds.

"That's helpful," said Morrison, "it still doesn't erase what tens of thousands of people have read. It doesn't make it go away."

Just then Constance arrived, having already read Brody's article. She looked down at the shreds of newspaper on the floor.

"Oh, I see you've read the article," said Constance, "I'm here to see what kind of damage control you want me to present at the press conference." Brody's article was worse than anything she had ever done. She could now appear the consummate ally.

"Leave me alone! All of you! Don't you have anything better to do than stand around here?" Lulu shouted ferociously as she grabbed her precious box and trudged up the stairs.

∽

Frank arrived at the precinct, ignorant of what had happened to his captain. He had not answered Marco's phone call and let it go to voicemail instead. Once inside he found everyone abuzz. Officers swiftly angled around cubicles and bounced off detectives like pinballs. The calls were coming in fast and furious as attested to by the continuous echo of ringing phones. *What's going on?* Frank made his way to the Special Unit and was bombarded by his fellow detectives.

"Frank, good to see you up and around again."

"Are you here because of Captain Dupree?"

"Isn't it just a shame, so close to retirement and all?"

"Do you know anything about this, you know, because of what happened to you?"

"STOP!" shouted Frank, "what are all of you talking about? *One* of you tell me what's going on around here. Where's the captain? I need to speak to him."

"Well, that's not going to happen."

"Yeah, the captain's dead."

"But how? What happened?" Frank was frozen in place, his eyes fully opened, while he waited for an answer.

"He was killed when his car flew over a cliff on Coast Highway."

Frank still paralyzed, ruminated on what he just heard. He knew the captain liked to drive that stretch of road to clear his mind and thoughts. And now that he had been enlightened with the reality of the Fifth Column,

Frank just knew they had to be involved, some way, somehow. He no longer felt safe there – or anywhere now for that matter. His basic instinct to flee kicked in and he pushed his comrades aside and ran out.

"Hey, Frank, where you goin'?" called an officer. But there was no response.

Marco and Martin pulled up as Frank ran out the front door. Frank hurriedly made his way toward them.

"Marco," said Frank, "have you heard about Dupree?"

"I know," Marco responded, "I tried calling you. Really sucks, doesn't it?"

"Worse than that, I don't think we should be seen here." Frank darted his gaze around the parking lot.

"*Now* who's the drama queen?" Marco laughed.

"No, really. I mean it. It's no laughing matter." Frank returned his focus to Marco.

"Okay. Calm down," Marco did his best to look serious. "Just let me get Martin on his way. We'll take your car back to Sara's. This Jag will draw too much attention. Go get your car from impound and meet me back here." Frank ran off to do just that.

Martin leapt out of his car when he saw his news van pull up. His cameraman jumped out and approached him.

"Martin," Marco called out, "you know what to do?"

"Yep," returned Martin, "tell the truth."

"Good," said Marco. He parked Martin's Jag and walked to the side of the building to wait for Frank. Frank's car approached so quickly that Marco plastered himself against the building in order to escape collision.

"Crap, Frank, I taught you to drive better than that."

"Just get in, Marco; I don't have a good feeling about any of this."

Marco got in the car and Frank sped off. Marco wondered if Frank was overly hysterical or if one of his gut feelings was actually going to pay off this time.

"Slow down, Frank, don't worry."

"Did you forget that Brody's article came out this morning? I didn't."

"Crap."

"Yeah, crap. We're twisting in the wind right now. We've got to get out of sight."

"Agreed. Let's light 'em up."

Frank slapped the blue LED strobe on top of his car, flipped on the siren and made tracks to Sara's.

❧

Winston came running into the house out of breath. He closed the door behind him and leaned on it in an attempt to regulate his breathing.

"Well?" asked Morrison.

"I know where they are," Winston stated between pants.

"Really? Where?"

"Over on Balboa at Twenty Seventh."

Lulu had heard the door and was descending the stairs when she heard Winston's news.

"Why that's just around the corner," she said, "those bastards!"

Constance, not a part of the conversation, went over and turned on the television to check the news. Within minutes there was a *Breaking News Report*. She saw none other than her nemesis center screen.

"Hey," beckoned Constance, "I think you'll want to see this. It can't be good. Martin is reporting on breaking news outside the police station."

"He's probably going to report on Dupree's death, that's all," said Morrison.

"We can't be so sure."

They all went over and stood in front of the television, some waiting for the other shoe to drop.

"This is Martin Jackson reporting from outside one of the SFPD's Special Unit division. Earlier this morning the captain of this unit, Captain Vincent Dupree, was found murdered at the bottom of a cliff off Coast Highway. Contrary to previous reports, this was not an accident but a serious act of violence brought on by a group of dangerous people residing right here in San Francisco. Fearing for my safety, as well as the safety of others, I am unable to comment any further on this group, only to say that an investigation is underway with Federal assistance now involved. This is Martin Jackson reporting."

"That's just great," said Lulu, "now I *know* you had something to do with this, Morrison."

"No way. You know I don't like to get my own hands dirty."

"Then you had someone do it *for* you."

"Who? Everyone else is either busy or dead. Well, except for you. You're neither, for the moment."

"It wasn't *me* you idiot!"

"Well, Lulu, doth ye protest too much?"

"Shut up, Morrison. I'll never believe you, but we've got more cleaning up to do now."

"I'll say."

"Excuse me," interrupted Constance, "did you guys hear the part where that idiot of a reporter said Federal agents are now involved in the investigation? What are we going to do about *that*?"

"We can't worry about that now," Lulu retorted.

"Well what am I going to say at the press conference?"

"Cancel it."

"That's the *first* good idea you've had," said Morrison.

"Really, genius? Like all your ideas have worked out so well," snapped Lulu, "like that last one with Dupree."

"I told you I had nothing to do with it."

"*Now* who protests too much?"

Roger came running into the living room excitedly flapping the papers gripped in his hand.

"We've completed the upload for NIPPER," he said, "I don't believe it, but we did it. Somehow we were able to stop the virus and reverse the damage."

"Well, finally some good news for a change," said Lulu.

"That's not all," continued Roger enthusiastically, "we're just about ready to breach SIPPER."

"About that," began Lulu, "I'd much rather you access CRONOS first. Let's see what NATO is up to these days."

"Oh yeah, the Cross Response Operations in NATO OS. Good one, but we'll have to go back and work out the encryption before we can breach it."

"Well *I* think it would be much wiser to first access the Intelink run by the CIA and their link to the White House. Let's see what intel our President is given and then check NATO's responses with CRONOS," said Morrison.

"Who cares what *you* think you pigheaded fool?" Lulu was irate at his daring to challenge her in front of everyone. *"I'm* in charge here and *I* say we go for the CRONOS connection."

"Wouldn't it be better to find out what the U.S. is thinking first? Then we could interrupt communications and send over our own false reports to NATO's command. The U.S. would be confused at their responses and take actions it wouldn't normally have taken," said Morrison.

Lulu didn't want to admit it but he was making sense.

"Roger, which process do you think you could breach quicker? CRONOS or the CIA's Intelink to the White House?"

Not sure if this was some sort of a trick, Roger decided to give the only answer he could, the truth.

"The CIA's Intelink would be quicker since we've already made access to part of the Intelink."

"Then do it," commanded Lulu. She turned to Morrison, "I'm going upstairs to email the change in plans. Let's hope you're not wrong on this one."

"I'm not," returned Morrison, feeling a rise in power.

Lulu retreated to the stairs and began her ascent but paused on the third step. She couldn't let Morrison believe he had any control of the situation. She turned back to face him.

"Oh, and don't think for one minute I'm going to give you any credit," she reminded him, making sure he knew who was in charge. Morrison's smile was transferred from his face to hers. Lulu erected herself more confidently, turned and went to notify her command.

"Winston," shouted Morrison, "get over here. I have a job for you."

Winston, feeling more self-assured after his latest accomplishment, walked fearlessly over to him.

"What is it?"

"I believe we are ready to send a more potent message to those interfering detectives."

"What do you have in mind?"

"How about some fireworks?" Morrison lowered his voice, "now that you've found the location where they've holed up, you can strap a bomb under their car. Then, *boom*, message sent."

"Good idea," said Winston, but he thought just the opposite. Now Morrison wanted a bomb to go off? He was just as bad as Lulu. But Winston was in, all the way in-and in too deep.

"I'm glad you see it my way," said Morrison, "let me get you the package." He walked over to a locked door just off the living room, opened it and disappeared inside.

Duncan retreated to the farthest corner of the living room in a fruitless attempt to hide. He looked over at Constance and their eyes locked. She just shook her head.

Morrison returned with a box and handed it to Winston. He whispered something to him and Winston exited the front door.

Duncan, seizing the opportunity while Morrison's back was to him, rushed out the back door. He had no idea why he did this and wasn't sure what he was going to do. He just wanted out – to escape. Once out on the street he saw Winston turn his car around and drive away. Duncan instinctively jumped in his car to follow. *What am I doing?* He asked himself, but the urge to follow was strong. Wherever Winston was about to take him, he had a feeling it would have a volatile impact on them all.

Mousetrap

Bradley was not feeling well-not at all. He decided that he would fight through his discomfort and make his way to the house on Fulton Street. But once in the foyer, his breathing became labored. A sudden piercing spasm shot down his left arm with an agonizing impact. He knew this wasn't good. Not wanting to leave himself unprotected, he painstakingly made his way to the credenza near the front door. Opening a side panel he reached for his gun and placed it inside his coat pocket. Now clutching his chest in anguish he reached for the phone on top of the credenza and dialed 911. All at once he was rendered speechless, fell to the floor and entered a painful darkness.

⁓

While Montgomery continued laboring on the computer, Darcy and Sara decided to relax and watch some television. A welcome peace had fallen upon the room.

"Would you like some more coffee, Darcy?" asked Sara.

"No thanks," returned Darcy, "I just want to get some rest." She lifted her legs up on the sofa and put her head to rest on the arm. Sara came over, offered her a pillow, sat down and turned on the TV.

"Oh, look," said Sara, "there's my Martin."

Darcy immediately sat up, her stillness broken, "turn it louder."

Sara raised the volume and the two listened intently.

Having overheard the reporter's story, Montgomery turned around to face the women.

"They're striking deep now," he said, "We've got to be much more vigilant. How safe do you think we are here?"

"According to Marco," began Darcy, "very safe. He said no one knows about Sara much less where she lives."

"That point will only buy us very little time. Let me finish what I'm doing here and then we'll talk more about it." He returned to his attempt of infiltrating and disabling the Fifth Column's computers.

"Did you know Captain Dupree?" Sara asked of Darcy.

"Not very well. He was Frank and Marco's captain."

"Oh, well it's still very sad."

"And I feel his death has put us in even much more danger."

"Just like in my books."

"No, Sara, this is *real*."

"What I write about is real."

"Were you ever in any of those situations yourself?"

"No, but. . . ."

"You are now. I can't impress upon you enough that we have inadvertently put you in a very dangerous position, and for that I am sorry."

"Okay, but it's not necessary to apologize, Darcy. Marco has brought trouble here before. But not *this* kind of trouble. What would you like me to do?"

"I think it would be best if you pack a bag and go stay at a hotel for a while. Why not treat yourself?"

"That sounds delightful. I've discovered that actually being in the line of fire really isn't very much fun anyway. Are you sure you don't need me?"

"Very sure. Now go pack."

Brody, having satisfied himself with yet another shower, bumped into Sara in the hallway.

"Where are you going in such a rush?" he asked.

"I'm going to treat myself to a vacation."

"Must be nice."

"It is." Sara glided into her room to prepare her escape.

Brody entered the living room. Montgomery was in deep concentration at the computer. Darcy was sitting on the sofa staring at a blank TV screen, with grave concern encompassing her countenance.

"Is Frank back yet?" he asked her.

"No, but I expect he'll be back soon," she looked directly at Brody, "Dupree's dead."

"What? How?"

"Murdered. He was found at the bottom of a cliff off Coast Highway."

"Whoa. That's bad."

"You have no idea. And we've complicated our predicament by pushing the envelope. Marco must have told Martin to lay it all out in his news report before the Fifth Column could give their abridged version of events to the public. That, plus your article, will put us directly in their sights."

"Is it too late to quit?"

"Why, Brody, you know better than that. And besides, I never pegged you for a defeatist."

"How about a chicken that wants to stay alive?"

"We can keep your neck off the chopping block. Don't worry; you've done well so far."

"Then can I at least have a gun?"

"Certainly not. We already have Butch and Sundance pointing their weapons at the drop of a hat and Wyatt Earp over there," she pointed to Montgomery, "ready at a moment's notice. So no, you don't need a gun."

"Okay, the decoder has retrieved the passcode," said Montgomery to no one in particular, "now I just need to send in the Trojan Horse. . . ." his voice trailed off.

"What?" asked Brody.

"Never mind him," said Darcy, "I don't understand much of it myself, but apparently he's loading the virus to the Fifth Column's computers."

"Score one for the good guys," exclaimed Brody. Darcy smiled. Brody liked it when she smiled. To him this meant that everything was going to turn out just fine.

Marco and Frank pulled up so furiously outside Sara's row house that Frank forgot the clutch, pressed the brake and stalled the car with a jerk.

"Good one," said Marco, "you wanna give me whiplash?"

"Shut up, Marco. Let's get inside."

The two men rushed inside, slammed the door and locked it.

"What did I tell you, Brody?" Darcy reiterated, "And in comes Butch and Sundance."

Not the least bit interested in her sarcasm, Marco had bigger things on his mind.

"Did you hear about Dupree?" he asked.

"Yep. Saw Martin's report on TV," said Darcy.

"How'd he do?"

"Well enough to want them to continue gunning for us."

"Good. That ought to keep them concentrating more on us and less on hacking their way to the top." Marco looked over at Montgomery, "how's he coming?"

"Quite well," said Darcy.

"Yeah, he's just about got the virus attacking," said Brody with excitement.

"Wow, little man, looks like you're finally getting into it," said Marco, "and do I detect an attitude adjustment has taken place, too?" Brody liked *this* Marco better. He decided to forgive him.

"Where's Sara?" asked Frank.

"She's going on vacation," informed Brody, enthusiastically.

"Well, not exactly. I've instructed her to go stay at a hotel," Darcy clarified, "I feel it's become too dangerous for her to remain here. She's in her room packing."

"Good," said Marco, "thanks, Darcy."

"No problem. We may need someone around to tell the truth of the matter, you know, in case we don't make it."

"Hey," protested Brody, "what am I?"

"Too close," said Darcy.

∾

Awakening to the steady beeping, Bradley fought through his stupor and came to realize that he was in the hospital. With fear welling up inside him he used every ounce of his strength to survey his surroundings. Monitors to his side were capturing all his vital signs and a single serpentine curtain was surrounding him. He heard people rushing and scuffling about through the thin protection; an urgency in their voices. He was still in the ER, he thought. Bradley turned his head to the other side and saw his clothes placed in a heap on a chair. His only thought was to seize his weapon. Slowly, slowly, he reached until he was able to grab on to the sleeve of his coat. Having spent all of his energy on this nearly insurmountable task, he fell back onto the bed, holding fast to the sleeve. After taking a few moments to catch his breath, he then reached into the pocket. Frantically he searched only to find it empty. His pulse raced as his focus turned to panic. But as a moment of calm came upon him, he suddenly realized he needed to check the other pocket. In what seemed an eternity, Bradley was able to turn the coat over until he had access to the other pocket. He reached inside and slid his feeble fingers around his gun. He sighed with relief. Carefully Bradley pulled out the gun, slid it under his sheet and covered it with the corner of his hospital gown. He closed his eyes as weakness returned. A nurse flung open the curtain and rushed over to the monitors. Noticing Bradley was stirring she addressed him.

"Mr. Ambrose, you're in the hospital. Don't try to move," she said while wondering who left his coat lying on top of him like that. She picked it up, folded it neatly and placed it on top of his other belongings in the chair. As she did so, Bradley opened his eyes and tried to speak but only managed groans and grunts.

"Don't try to talk, Mr. Ambrose. You've had a massive stroke," she said. "You'll need some therapy before you can speak again-you'll be fine though."

But Bradley didn't believe her. *I'll never be fine again,* he thought. This was all just too much for him.

"We're moving you to a private room now," she said as she injected something into his IV feed, "you will be staying in this bed so close your eyes and get some rest."

Bradley tried to fight the drug but it was too powerful, just like the Fifth Column, just like Morrison . . . and he drifted off to an agitated and uneasy sleep.

∽

Captain Morrison, having given his orders to Winston, decided it was time to check in on Bradley. He was growing weary of being his babysitter.

He decided he was going to stop coddling him. Morrison pulled out his cell phone and dialed Bradley at home, but someone else picked up.

"Who's this? Where's Ambrose?" Morrison gruffly inquired.

"Who's this?" the voice returned.

"This is Captain Morrison of the SFPD and I demand to speak to Bradley Ambrose."

"Oh, uh, well, he's been taken to the hospital. A heart attack or something."

Captain Morrison hung up on whoever it was. Now Bradley had done it, he was finished as far as Morrison was concerned. If the heart attack hadn't already killed him, Morrison would see to it that *he* would put an end to Bradley's miserable life. He had grown tired of having to deal with the likes of this feeble-minded and weak little man, besides; the Fifth Column could manage without him now that they were well on their way to success. Then, after Bradley was taken care of, all that would be necessary would be for Morrison to eliminate Lulu and he'd be set. Set for the rest of his life.

∾

Winston parked back at Twenty-Fifth Street, took out the box and began his walk toward the house where the detectives were hiding.

Duncan pulled into a space a few cars down from where Winston had parked. He got out of his car to follow Winston who was now on foot. Unfortunately for Duncan, Winston was continually surveilling his surroundings and he had to drop farther and farther back to avoid detection.

Winston stopped when he reached a car parked directly in front of the domicile that sequestered his worthy adversaries. The car was obvious to spot for in his haste Frank had forgotten to remove the dome light atop his car. Duncan set the box down on the curb at the back of the car and stood up. He pushed the box under the car with his foot. Taking one last look around, he walked out into the street on the driver's side, dropped to the ground and slid under the car.

Duncan had only looked away for what he thought was a moment and he lost sight of Winston. Dare he move closer? Just then a resident came walking out from one of the buildings carrying an overstuffed box of belongings. *Obviously moving out*, he thought. He noticed it was a woman, a very pretty one in fact, who was struggling to maintain balance in her effort to get herself and the box safely down the stairs. Deciding to be chivalrous, Duncan came to her aid.

"Thank you," she said, "I didn't realize I'd stuffed the box so full."

"That happens," said Duncan, "here, let me help you." And he grabbed one side of the box and they lowered it. The closer he was, he could now see that she was extraordinarily beautiful. Under very different circumstances he most likely would have pursued her. Damn shame, too.

"Where would you like it?" he asked.

"Just set it here, next to my car. I'll put it in later when I've brought down more boxes." She waited for an offer of further assistance. But Duncan had turned his attention back to where he'd last spotted Winston. Winston was there facing toward a house that seemed to be holding his interest. Duncan watched as Winston smiled and gave a haphazard salute in its direction. With no time left to contemplate Winston's strange behavior, Duncan watched as Winston turned to go back to his car.

"Ya know," began Duncan hurriedly as he took the woman's arm and directed her back toward her door, "I can help with a few more boxes if you'd like."

"Why sure. That would be great," she returned. They both walked up the stairs, Duncan nearly dragging her, and entered her building just as Winston quickly passed by.

After bringing down several loads of boxes, Duncan purposefully looked at his watch.

"Wow, I didn't realize the time. I've got to be going now."

"Well thank you for your help," she said, "Would you. . ." but Duncan was already two doors down the street taking long strides toward the house Winston had previously saluted.

❧

Sara entered the living room and placed a large suitcase by the door.

"I'm ready," she reported, "at least I think I am. In a situation like this, well, I'm just a little bit scattered."

Suddenly there was a knock at the door.

"I'll get it," said Sara, suddenly oblivious to their danger.

"NO!" shouted the officers collectively.

"Oh my, now I can't wait to get out of here," said Sara.

"Back up," commanded Darcy, "over in the hallway," she motioned with her head.

Montgomery was on his feet with the rest of them. Darcy held up her hand to them, unholstered her gun and moved to the door. Brody, still not accustomed to any of this, moved back into the hallway with Sara.

Darcy grabbed the handle of the door with her left hand while she hid her gun in her right hand behind her back. Slowly opening the door, she addressed the young man standing there.

"Can I help you?" she cautiously asked.

"Not really, well maybe, but *I* can help *you*," said Duncan.

"Really?"

"Do you know Brody Abernathy?"

"Hey," yelled Brody, "that's Duncan!"

After Brody's outburst, Darcy flung open the door and pulled Duncan in so swiftly that he tumbled to the floor. Darcy slammed the door behind her.

"Why are you here?" she demanded an answer.

Duncan looked up to see four guns pointed directly at him. Brody rushed over and stood next to Marco, gloating.

"Hah, you dumbass. You're in trouble now," asserted Brody.

"No," said Duncan, "actually *you* are. That's why I'm here, to warn you."

"Don't trust him! It's a trick I tell you," alerted Brody as he commenced toward Duncan. Marco grabbed hold of his shirt before he could reach him.

"Don't make me ruin a perfectly good shirt," said Marco, "it's one of my favorites." He turned to Duncan, "now why are you *really* here?"

"It's like I said, to save you. Captain Morrison and Lulu have gone crazy."

"How?" asked Montgomery?

"They're acting very strange, even for them. Things seem to be getting way out of control. It's hard to tell who's in charge anymore."

Frank went over to Duncan, pulled him up and checked him for weapons "He's clean," he reported.

They all put their weapons away.

"Now what was it you said about us being in trouble?" asked Darcy.

"Well, Captain Morrison ordered Winston to come over here and send you a message."

"How do they know we're here?" asked Marco.

"Winston followed one of you over here this morning after he saw your car pass their house."

Brody shot a glance at Marco and Frank while Darcy felt Montgomery's stare blazing into her soul; all of them equally harboring possible guilt. Wanting to skip this part of the conversation, Darcy jumped in.

"What kind of message do they want to send us?"

"I can't say for sure, but Winston was out front just a while ago looking at this house. That's how I found you. That and the police car out front."

"What makes you think that's a police car?" asked Darcy.

"Well, for one, there's some kind of a dome light on the roof," Duncan informed her.

"Crap," said Marco as he turned to Frank, "what the hell?"

"Okay, so I made a mistake. Like *you've* never made one?"

"Not one that lit up like a neon sign saying, 'they're in here, come and get them'. Geez, Frank, you know the gravity of the situation."

"Alright," said Darcy, "Frank screwed up, he's sorry. Let's move on, shall we?"

"Sounds good to me," said Frank.

"It would," said Marco.

"STOP IT!" yelled Darcy, "You two are beginning to sound like an old married couple." The two of them just stared at her. "That's better."

Duncan took a small step back. He couldn't believe his luck in walking into another bickering battle. He surmised they weren't much different from how the Fifth Column was operating at the moment. His eyes trailed from one person to the other, feeling vulnerable once again. Rocking from foot to foot, side to side, he felt he was along for yet another wild ride.

"So if what Duncan says is true, then none of us are safe here any longer," said Frank, a new urgency resonating in his voice, "we've all got to go, now."

"I can't leave just yet," said Montgomery, "I'm not quite finished with what I'm doing here. I just need a few more minutes."

Duncan, remembering he had proof of the Fifth Column's conspiracy on his cell phone, reached in his pocket to pull it out. Noticing this, the officers immediately reached for their weapons. Duncan instinctively held his arms in the air.

"Marco, go see what he has in his pocket," commanded Darcy.

Marco approached Duncan and carefully reached in his pocket and retrieved a cell phone.

"See, I told you it was a trick," said Brody, "he's going to call them right now!"

"You really are a douche, Brody. If I was going to call the Fifth Column, why would I be so obvious? Huh?"

"Then why *were* you reaching for your phone?" asked Darcy.

"I was going to show you something I discovered about Lulu and the people she reports to, that's all."

"I'll take that," said Montgomery and he snatched the cell phone away from Marco and put it in his pocket, "no time to deal with that now. The rest of you get out of here and I'll stay and finish."

"Marco, you take Duncan, Sara and Brody to the warehouse," ordered Darcy, "Frank and I will stay here until Montgomery's done. We'll meet you there." Marco began to protest, "This is no time to argue, now go."

Frank tossed his keys to Marco and the four of them walked quickly out the door toward the car. Duncan was so rattled by their behavior he had completely forgotten that Winston had also left something behind.

"Oh, shoot, I forgot my purse," Sara snapped her fingers. She abruptly turned back toward the house.

"There's no time," said Marco but it was too late, she was already inside. Turning to Brody, "go get her and bring her back out here."

Brody, following orders, rushed back into the house while Marco and Duncan got in the car. Almost immediately Marco saw Brody dragging Sara out of the house, her retrieved purse waving behind her.

"Come on, Sara, we've got to go," Brody urged.

"I know and let go of me," rebelled Sara.

Marco put the key in and turned the ignition but only heard a screech.

"What now?" asked Marco.

"The clutch," said Duncan.

"I knew that."

"Sure."

Brody and Sara had nearly reached the car when Marco started the engine. They were suddenly propelled back by a concussion, landing backside on the ground. Flames immediately erupted from underneath the car and plumes of smoke were sent hurling upwards. The flames grew with ferocity and began whipping its entirety until the car was barely visible. The smoky haze turned into a dark, dense fog as it consumed the vehicle.

"Smoke!" Sara screamed as she began to rise, waving her arms to exact a clear view of the image before her.

Brody, his body now wrapped in intense heat, raised up his head. He didn't want to believe what he was looking at. He closed his eyes. *Make it go away.*

ৎ৽

Captain Morrison was at the nurse's station demanding information.

"Where is Bradley Ambrose's room?"

"He's resting right now," said the nurse, "perhaps you can come back later."

"No. I need to see him now."

Having taken note of his uniform she asked, "Is this a police matter?"

"That's not your concern. Now where is Mr. Ambrose?"

"My concern is for Mr. Ambrose. He's not well enough for visitors. You'll have to come back later."

"Perhaps I'm not making myself clear enough. I'm going to see Bradley Ambrose, and you're going to tell me where to find him."

The nurse pressed a hidden button under the desk to alert security. She feared for her safety and the safety of the patients. So as a way of not alerting him to her concern, she decided to oblige him.

"He's in room 423."

"Now was that so difficult?" Morrison patronized, and he was off to find Bradley to tie up the latest loose end.

Having heard the explosion, Darcy and Frank reached the front door with lightning speed. What they witnessed was a dreadful scene with Frank's car fully engulfed in flames. An intensity of heat washed upon them. Frank frantically looked for signs of Marco while Darcy ran to the aid of Brody and Sara who were attempting to rise from their prone positions.

Neighbors appeared from their homes, curiously aghast at the sight. Some could be seen on cell phones frantically waving their arms and yelling. A few cautiously approached the scene.

"Marco!" yelled Frank. There was no response. He rushed toward the car and was overcome by a thick cloud of smoke; the heat emanating from his car, now lit up like a torch, was too extreme and prevented any further advancement. In his distress he fell to his knees, put his head in his hands and broke down.

"Brody, Sara, are you two alright?" yelled Darcy over the sound of the roaring flames and the popping and hissing of destruction. She reached over to assist them maintain balance as they stood up.

"Marco. Where's Marco?" called Sara, looking to Darcy for reassurance.

"I'm sorry," conferred Darcy as sympathetically as she could, still numb.

"NO, NO, NO," wailed Sara. She began to sob and fell trembling into Darcy's arms.

Brody stood there in disbelief, partly because Marco and Duncan were incinerated along with Frank's car and partly because he had been only moments away from joining them. Too many emotions were fighting within him, and he wasn't able to make a lock on any of them. All at once his cheeks became stained with tears, his body shook and the color drained from his face. He looked over to see Sara convulsively weeping on Darcy. His focus then turned to a howling sound of suffering like he'd never heard before. He looked toward the sound and found Frank on his knees rocking back and forth in pain. Not a physical pain that can be healed, but a pain so deep that can never be overcome.

"BRODY," Darcy shouted, "Brody, snap out of it. Come here and take care of Sara while I check on Frank."

Almost robotically Brody approached the two women.   Darcy unclenched Sara's grip and pushed her toward Brody. He instinctively held out his arms and Sara fell into them.

Darcy ran toward the flames, captivated by its power. Her face became flushed and the closer she got to the flaming wreckage, the more she perspired. She brushed away the fallen locks of hair that now covered her face and surveyed the carnage. Side-stepping around the car she was horrified at the sight. Suddenly she heard a lamenting sound break through the din of the turbulence. She came around the vehicle to find Frank still on the ground overcome with anguish.

"Frank," said Darcy softly as she put her hand to rest on his shoulder, "Come on. There's nothing you can do."

"But Marco . . . I can't find Marco."

"I know, Frank."

Captain Morrison arrived at Bradley's room. He paused to contemplate which approach he should take to complete Bradley's demise. He walked over to the clamoring monitors. *Too obvious*, he thought. That would just bring all the staff upon them in a matter of moments. He continued to scan the room but did not find anything of much use for his purpose. He looked at Bradley. How pitiful and weak he looked, *this will be too easy*. But some days it's just like that, everything seems to go your way. Bradley didn't appear to be aware of Morrison's presence. Morrison watched as Bradley's chest rose and fell with each breath; a breath that will soon be taken from him. Morrison walked over to a nearby closet and opened it. Inside were extra pillows and blankets. He grabbed one of the pillows and pulled it down. Taking hold of each end, he slowly approached Bradley.

Bradley was not asleep; in fact he was every bit aware of Morrison. He listened very carefully to each step Morrison was taking, closer, closer. Bradley clutched his gun tightly in his right hand. He was glad he had the foresight to arm himself; he was wise not to trust them, especially Morrison.

Captain Morrison had reached the right side of Bradley's bed, still no visible signs of movement. *Like fish in a barrel.*

"Good night, Bradley," he muttered while lowering the pillow over Bradley's face, "it's been a real pleasure." And he quietly snickered to himself as he pushed the pillow down over Bradley's face with all his force.

Bradley, knowing time was now fleeting, trained the gun in Morrison's direction. With every ounce of strength he had remaining he used it to pull the trigger.

The pain shot through Morrison like a bolt of lightning. He let go of the pillow and put his hands on his now bloodstained uniform. With his final breaths now upon him Morrison became incredulous that Bradley had bested him - even in his condition.

"You bastard," cursed Morrison as blood began to rise in his throat and seep out of his mouth. With a last rush of adrenaline he reached for Bradley's neck, but that was all he had left in him. His final essence succumbed to his wound and he fell over on top of Bradley. Just then the monitors seized and all that could be heard was a steady hum.

ҩ

Montgomery used every bit of concentration he had left to complete his task. He would have to let Darcy and Frank handle the situation outside until he was finished loading the virus to the Fifth Column's computers. Putting distraction out of his mind, he was soon finished and removed the flash drive. Shoving it in his pocket he hurried toward the door. What he saw in front of him was nothing short of devastation. He paused for a moment to take it all in. He knew the Fifth Column was deadly serious, but now it touched him on a personal level. Montgomery never let this happen before; to become personally involved like this. He was always able to keep his distance, remain detached and focused. But this eclectic group of people with their passion for justice, well, he just couldn't help but become fascinated with them. And an unusual sorrow crept into his heart, and for a moment, he let it lead him.

✺

"Lulu," Roger shouted, "where are you?"

"What on Earth is wrong with you?" she asked while descending the stairs. Already angry she hadn't received a response from her command regarding the change in plans, she did not want to have to deal with the hysterics of this little geek.

"What is it, Roger?" she asked sternly.

Afraid of her ever increasing irritability, but more afraid of being unsuccessful, he decided to fill her in on the latest disaster.

"We've got another problem. A *bigger* one this time."

"How bad is it?"

"Real bad. A much stronger virus is now challenging our efforts. It's destroying everything it can attach itself to."

"Well, fix it."

"We're working on that. But with every keystroke it grows stronger. Very soon it will disable us."

"Why are you just standing there then? Get over there and stop it!"

Realizing she was not comprehending what he was saying and knowing she would just become more agitated with any further pursuit of an explanation, Roger went back to his computer and shut it down.

"What are you doing?" asked Marta.

"The only thing I can do at the moment."

"Why aren't you fighting this?"

"It's a losing battle."

"No it's not. Come here and take a look at this."

Roger didn't believe she could possibly do more on her lowly computer than he had already done on his quantum computer with all its power and safeguards. But maybe that was it. Maybe there was so much involved with his computer that it was rendered more vulnerable. It was an interesting theory. He decided to see if Marta was on to something, but by the time he reached her desk, her computer was running useless algorithms on its own. *They were doomed.*

In the other room Constance was watching as Lulu contemplated her next move.

"Lulu, what are we going to do now?"

"Hold on and let me think, will you?" Lulu sniped.

Having grown immune to Lulu's disagreeable disposition, Constance queried further, "What if they can't recover our computers this time?"

"That is *not* an option."

༄

The shrill sound of sirens in the distance began and overshadowed the small explosions emanating from the smoldering wreckage. Police cars hastily rolled up, stopping just beyond Frank's car, now almost completely unrecognizable. Neighbors jumped out of the way of approaching ambulances and the fire trucks slowly edged their way to the scene. The once quiet and peaceful neighborhood had now become ground zero for tragedy and despair. A police officer, recognizing Frank, approached him for answers.

"Frank, are you okay?" inquired the officer, "can you tell me what happened here?"

With suddenness, Frank's emotion turned to fury. He stood up and confronted the mass of people now gathered around him.

"Why are you all just standing there? We've got to help them. Why is nobody helping them?" he pleaded through tears of anguish, "do something!"

"Frank, think about this," Darcy spoke with evenness, "they're gone. Marco's gone."

"No," protested Frank and he pushed her, "you're wrong!"

"She's right, Frank," yelled Montgomery from the top of the steps, "listen to her."

"What do you know G-man? Huh? Were you out here?" Frank screamed with great depth of emotion.

"I was," cried Brody, "it's true. They were inside the car."

"Frank, my Marco's gone. Can't you see that?" Sara pleaded tearfully, "I saw him and then he was gone!" Sara had found her reality.

Shaking his head and taking it all in, Frank turned to Darcy. "Well what should we do now? We can't let them get away with this!"

"And we won't," Darcy stated with certainty.

Montgomery walked down the stairs and approached them. "I've disabled their computers," he said, "now let's disable *them*."

"Good idea," agreed Frank, "Let's go." And he absently turned to make his leave.

"Wait a minute," pressed Darcy, "we need a plan first,"

"Yeah. *My* plan is to kill every one of them. That's what *I* plan to do," Frank angrily shouted at them.

"Vengeance is only a momentary drug," Montgomery pointed out, "we need a permanent cure. Let's do as Darcy says. Let's create a plan."

"Well, we know where they are," said Frank slowly returning to them and to his senses.

"That's a good place to start," said Darcy.

"And they'll expect us to be so caught up in what's happened here that we'll delay any aggressive action," said Montgomery.

"We can still have an element of surprise," added Darcy, "they're only a few blocks away from here. We can just walk right up there and take them."

"That's ambitious," Brody momentarily stepped outside his grief.

"You bet it is. We can afford that luxury now," said Darcy. "Okay, so this is how it's going to play out," she looked toward Brody and Sara, "you two stay here and lock yourselves inside. Brody, I'm serious. I don't want to find you skulking behind us, understand?"

"Yes," he said feeling somewhat dejected he was told he wouldn't be allowed to participate.

"That's good for me," said Sara, "I don't think I could handle much more right now anyway."

"Good," said Darcy.

"So, what *are* we going to do?" asked Frank.

"The three of us are going to take a little walk."

"I like the way you think, Darcy," Montgomery expressed in the most professional manner possible.

"Me too," Frank concurred, hopefulness now resonating through his words, "and thanks for helping me, well, you know."

"I know, Frank," Darcy returned, accompanied by a smile filled with warmth.

Then with a great purpose in mind, the three of them, Darcy, Frank and Montgomery, took off on foot toward the house on Fulton Street; leaving the local authorities to wade through the destruction.

Brody waited until they were out of sight and then headed down the front steps toward the street.

"Where are you going?" asked Sara, "didn't you hear what Darcy said?"

"Yeah, so? She knows I rarely ever listen to her anyway. She won't care once I get there. And besides, what's she going to do about it?"

"Really? You think she isn't going to care that you disobeyed her? That you put yourself in harms' way? She sounded serious, Brody. She might even shoot you."

"She always talks that way to me, but I know she likes me, deep down inside somewhere."

"I don't know, Brody. I think you're reading her all wrong."

"No way. Now go lock yourself inside."

"No way to *you*. You're not leaving me here alone." And Sara walked to the sidewalk to help settle the score.

Checkmate

Lulu had made up her mind and was ready to pass final judgment on her current assignment, which was quickly spiraling out of her control and beyond reconciliation. Without consulting those in charge of the Fifth Column beforehand, she began putting a plan in motion, one she was uncertain they would have approved. For this reason she felt great concern. She had always been their perfect "little soldier" but had she stepped out of line this time? Had she failed to live up to the demands placed on her? Was she too hasty with some of her decisions when she let Morrison get under her skin? Lulu realized Morrison had made her flinch, and by doing so, had allowed him too much rope. He was running amok and slipshod over her organization. She was furious with herself for allowing this to happen and thus she felt as if failure was eminent. Bottom line: it was her responsibility to make sure the operation in San Francisco was successful, and she didn't see much chance of that happening now.

One of her worst mistakes though was not recognizing Montgomery for the traitor he was. But she had not chosen him, she reasoned, it was her superiors who had sent him to San Francisco to assist her in her efforts. He was to make sure her operation was not compromised. She now knew it was Montgomery that had been compromising them all along. At every turn she had allowed him complete access to do so. And wherever he was now it appeared that he was continuing in his efforts to bring her down. This time he had delivered a slam-dunk virus to their computers; she could hear it in Roger's voice. She knew she didn't understand Roger much of the time, but she understood the look on his face. Deep down she knew they would never recover from this latest setback. And besides, their location had been jeopardized. There was only one thing left to do.

Winston returned to the house from his latest assignment. Seeing only Lulu, he asked, "Where's Morrison?"

"I haven't seen him," she replied, "why? Is there something I can help you with?"

"Not really. It's just that I'm done with what he asked me to do, that's all."

"And what was that?"

"Send another message to those cops."

"I see. What great idea did he come up with this time?"

Not sure what her reaction would be for following instructions from Morrison, he was hesitant to explain the details of his plan.

"Go ahead. You can tell me," Lulu slyly stated.

Seeing no way out now, and with Lulu technically his boss, he decided to reveal what he had been up to.

"Morrison had me plant a bomb under one of their cars," he rattled off quickly.

"So *that's* what I heard."

"Yep."

"I have an idea," she said with certainty, "come with me." And Lulu took him to the door just off the living room, unlocked it and they went inside.

പ്ര

Darcy, Frank and Montgomery had just concluded their walk down Twenty-Seventh and arrived at the corner of Fulton Street. They paused for a moment to go over their plan one more time. But Darcy became awash with an uneasy feeling and out of the corner of her eye she noticed a young couple following them. She turned to get a better look but they were no longer there. She saw nothing but the rustling of some bushes.

"Wait here," she told them, "I'm going to check on something." They waited and watched as she walked back up Twenty-Seventh. They saw her stop abruptly, turn toward an overgrown hedge and begin speaking.

"Alright you two, get up. I thought I told you to lock yourselves in the house. What happened?"

"Brody was going to leave me alone," answered Sara, "I was too petrified to stay there."

"I can't believe you just ratted me out. That's a woman for ya," said Brody.

"Ahem," sounded Darcy.

"Oh, well not *you*. I don't really think of you as a woman. Wait. What I mean is you're a cop and not a real woman . . . uh, like other women. Oh, hell, forget it."

"Let's do," said Darcy, "I don't suppose it would do me any good to send you back to the house would it?"

"Not really," Brody attested while he rose to a standing position.

"And I'm not going by myself," added Sara while she stood up as straight as she could.

"Okay," said Darcy and she grabbed Brody's arm, "you're coming with me."

"I'm not coming with you," protested Brody. But Darcy yanked harder on his arm, pulling him along, "I guess I am."

Once they reached the corner Frank was livid at the sight of Brody and Sara.

"What the hell, Brody? Isn't it bad enough you always find a way to interfere with our business, but did you have to drag Sara along too?"

"*That* was *my* idea," said Sara.

"Does your brain have the same capacity as his?" Frank insulted her; incredulous she had the nerve to respond.

"Well probably more but . . . oh, you meant that as rhetorical . . . sorry."

"Maybe you don't realize this, Frank," began Brody, "but I didn't sign up for this . . . you guys keep dragging me into this thing, *literally!*"

"Perhaps you two may not understand the grave importance of what we are about to do and the serious danger involved," Montgomery warned, "we have enough to focus on without having to worry about you two as well."

"Yeah, you're gonna get us killed," sniped Frank.

"Well, maybe not that far, but we can't be distracted right now," implored Darcy, "however, since you have your heart set on following us, and you're already here, do you think you can stay back behind us and out of our way?"

"I can," Brody stoically agreed while secretly excited.

"For sure," added Sara seriously, realizing she was relinquishing complete control over to them.

"And if anything happens . . . anything bad . . . I want both of you to get the hell out of here," Darcy admonished, "understand?"

"I do," said Brody.

"I do," said Sara.

"I now pronounce you Idiot and Idiot," said Frank, "can we go now?"

"In a second," said Darcy, "I just want to recap. I will walk past the perimeter of the house, Montgomery will move back around the house and Frank, you'll go to the front door. Have we all got it?" They both nodded. "Then let's do it."

༄

Once inside the room, Lulu approached a wall that was lined with wooden crates stacked nearly to the ceiling. She located one at the bottom marked 'Finis'.

"Winston," she said, "take all these crates down and get me this one." She pointed to her selection.

Winston - with all his might - carefully unloaded each crate to the ground. While he was attending to his latest chore, Lulu had time to reflect on what was about to happen. Finis, or Finish. This crate contained materials only to be used in the final destruction of evidence upon completion of their task. She was to leave no witnesses and return back to the Fifth Column's overseas command post. But there was to be no completion, she would have to start over somewhere else. She had allowed too much infiltration, destruction, betrayal and death to be able to continue her business here. Years of careful planning and execution had dissolved right in front of her. She had no other choice.

"Here it is," said Winston as he placed the crate at her feet.

Retrieving a crowbar, she pried the top off the crate. Lulu then studied the contents and picked up one of the devices. She recalled the training she received on how they were to be executed.

"Let me show you how to prepare these," said Lulu. Winston moved closer and listened carefully as she described every detail on how to set the bomb.

"I want you to put one upstairs, one in the living room and one in the kitchen. Understand?"

"Yes," said Winston, curious at this new turn of events.

"No one is to see what you're doing. Just act as if you're checking on things, you are a maintenance man after all. None of them will be the wiser. Got it?"

"Yes."

"I will hand you one at a time. Set the first one upstairs for twenty minutes, the living room for fifteen minutes and the kitchen for ten minutes. When you're done, come back here to this room and report to me." She handed him the first device. "I'm going upstairs to pack some documents and put them in your car. May I have your keys?" Winston, remaining puzzled, reached in his pocket and handed them to her. "Now let's get busy, shall we?"

Seeing them exit the room, Constance was eager for something to do, anything to make use of the nervous energy she was restraining.

"Lulu, is there anything I can help you with?" offered Constance.

"As a matter of fact you can help me gather some papers that I need to transfer to my office," Lulu answered, "come upstairs with me."

Winston, having already fled up to the second floor, chose a front room to place the explosive. Lulu and Constance went up the stairs to a room across the hall where Lulu's computer and all her notes and papers were kept. Lulu instructed Constance to pack up some insignificant files while she stuffed the contents of her precious metal box into her briefcase, including the gun. The two women then carried the haul to Winston's car and placed it in the back seat.

"Thanks, Constance," said Lulu, "now wait in the living room. I'll have something else for you to do shortly."

They went back inside just as Winston was descending the stairs. Lulu met him back in the room and handed him another device.

"This one's for the living room," she ordered.

"But Constance is in there," Winston reminded her.

"I'll take care of it." She yelled out the door, "Constance, would you make some coffee?"

"Sure," Constance responded and proceeded to the kitchen to prepare a pot.

Winston then made a clear shot across the living room. He located an end table in the corner to place the second device. He was nearly finished setting the timer when Constance approached.

"What are you doing?" she inquired.

Having just completed the final steps to go live with the bomb, Winston rose to respond.

"I'm just checking all the connections to make sure we don't have any more problems with the computers," he said.

"Oh, well that's good. We certainly don't need any more setbacks - not now. Roger and Marta just rebooted their computers." And she dropped herself into the lumpy chair and waited for further instructions from Lulu.

Winston went back to the room and Lulu handed him the third and final device. He then went to the kitchen, opened the pantry and went in to set the bomb.

Lulu waited impatiently for Winston to finish. She twirled the keys on her fingers as she paced the small room. *This was it.* She harbored no doubts with relation to what she was about to do. She was on an adrenaline rush and was ready to go.

Winston bolted back into the room. "All done. Let's go," he said, "want me to get the others?"

"No, not yet," Lulu calmly enunciated as she closed the door and picked up the crowbar, "There's just one more thing." She pointed to a crate. While Winston turned to look she raised up the crowbar and landed it in the center of his skull with the potency of all her force. Having achieved its effectiveness, Winston's mass was instantly deposited on the floor in front of her. Blood slowly seeped from his wound and soaked into the carpet. Lulu dropped the crowbar, hurried out of the room and locked the door. She still had to remove one more obstacle.

"Constance," she began, "how about making some sandwiches for our hungry little techies? They've got lots of work to do and I don't want them passing out in the process."

"Sure, no problem," said Constance, "do you want one?"

"No. I'm going to drop off the papers at my office. I'll get something along the way."

"What about Winston?"

"No. He's busy."

Constance retreated to the kitchen and Lulu retreated - out the front door.

While driving away, she spotted Brody and three others walking rapidly down the street. It was all she could do to control herself, to keep from running them all down. But they were headed in the direction of the house. They'd be well taken care of there.

❧

"Hey," yelled Brody, "that was Lulu! She's getting away!"

Frank abruptly turned and grabbed hold of Brody by his shirt.

"What's wrong with you?" Frank reacted while angrily shaking him, "I oughta kick your ass right here."

Brody scrunched his face, waiting for an inevitable blow. But it never came. Frank felt Darcy's hand on his arm.

"Frank," she said.

"I know. I know. We've got more important things to do than for me to wrestle with this impudent, meddling, little imbecile," he spat as he released his grip on Brody.

"Look, Frank, I'm upset about Marco too, but don't take it out on me," Brody pointed out.

Frank realized Brody was making sense but he refused to apologize for his behavior. Brody's interference was causing them to waste valuable time - time that could be spent avenging Marco's death. Frank turned to Brody.

"Keep your mouth shut you little turd or I'll break your jaw," he hissed. Suddenly Frank was acting a lot like Marco and Duncan all rolled into one.

"Okay," Brody whined, "I just got caught up in the moment, seeing Lulu take off like that."

"Well get control of yourself for God's sake and let us do our jobs," Frank retorted.

"I want to do my part too," said Brody, relentless in his pursuit of justice, and a story too. "Can I have a gun now? I'd really feel safer with one."

Just as Darcy was about to respond, three consecutive blasts were heard down the street. The impact shook the ground, and they all struggled to maintain their balance. Turning toward the thunderous claps, they witnessed huge clouds of thick, dark smoke instantaneously ascending at an accelerated rate. At once they ran toward the detonation only to find that the little house on Fulton Street, the one that was to reveal all its secrets, had erupted in flames. Any hope for revenge was being eliminated before their eyes.

"I guess I just saved your lives," Brody indicated. "If it wasn't for me following you, you'd all be in there."

Brody was right again, thought Frank, perhaps there was a reason for keeping him around. Sara hugged Brody and gave him a kiss on the cheek. Darcy nodded and Montgomery patted Brody on the back. They all knew what he said was true and they were grateful this time for his annoying interference.

~

Darcy wanted them all to meet where this had all begun for her, the café in North Beach. Coming full circle would be both poignant and cathartic for her. All of them had taken this extraordinary, horrifying, exhilarating and heartbreaking journey together. She wanted them to be there with her, if only to make it all seem real.

It was late in the evening and a cool breeze was gently blowing. Darcy seated herself on the café's patio. They were serving up their most popular alcoholic beverage; Irish coffee. She savored the aroma of the coffee and relaxed as the Irish whiskey warmed her senses; the Irish crème added a richness that soothed her soul. Darcy was sitting at the same table where she had first run into Marco and Brody. She sipped slowly on her Irish coffee and she thought back to when Marco had gotten the best of her perp; the two of them rolling around on the floor. She could laugh about it now.

"What's so funny?" Brody asked, interrupting her thoughts.

"I was just thinking about you . . . and Marco."

Brody reached down, wrapped his arms around her and hugged tightly. Darcy just looked at him and smiled. He let go and sat down next to her.

"You've grown up, Brody, I hope you know that."

"Well I think you had a lot to do with it. And, Marco . . . in his own way."

"No, don't sell yourself short. You really stepped up when we needed you to. And you were there, all the way."

"I can't say I was always a willing participant, but yes, I did learn a lot about myself, about making friends and staying alive, that's for sure. It all seems like a long time ago. You were going to arrest me, right here," he laughed.

"I wasn't kidding either."

"I didn't think you were, but I had to challenge you anyway."

"That you did, paperboy, but Marco. . . ." a knot welled up in her throat. She was unable to continue as her eyes became pools filled with tears that wouldn't fall.

"I know," said Brody, understanding just how she felt, "I miss him too. He was not always nice to me, but I know he didn't mean it, not really. I'm sure I'm not the easiest person to get along with. Sometimes I guess I just try too hard, and maybe get in the way, and carry on about things too much, but I don't believe I was irritating and bothersome like he said I was."

"I know, Brody. It took me a while to warm up to your charms too."

"Hey," said Montgomery while approaching them, "is this where our little band of heroes is meeting?" He spotted a waitress and pointed to Darcy's glass, "three more please."

"Montgomery," said Darcy, "I'm glad you could make it."

"I wasn't really sure if I could, but I postponed my flight until tomorrow," he said as he sat down in the other seat next to Darcy. He reached inside his coat pocket and produced Darcy's transient scarf, "I believe this is yours," and handed it to her.

"You had my scarf all this time?" Darcy was unable to conceal her astonishment.

"Well, quite by accident, I assure you," returned Montgomery, "I had forgotten about it altogether once we got tangled up in the Fifth Column's affairs. But when I put my coat on this evening, I put my hand in my pocket and there it was."

"I had forgotten all about it myself. I haven't had much time to coordinate my wardrobe lately, you know, dodging bullets and bombs can be a bit distracting."

"Completely understandable," Montgomery concurred.

She was just about to ask him about his next assignment when a cab pulled up and a drunken Frank stumbled out. Montgomery went over to retrieve him, paid the cabbie and deposited Frank in the chair next to Brody.

"Hey everybody," Frank slurred, "I started without you. But, hey, I'm here."

Montgomery flagged for the attention of their waitress, "one very strong black coffee, please."

"Coffee?" asked Frank, "could you put a little something in it?"

"Cream will be fine," said Montgomery.

During their brief silence the waitress returned and served the Irish coffees to everyone but Frank.

"Damn," groaned Frank as the waitress placed a plain cup of coffee in front of him.

"Frank, we're all drinking coffee, see?" and Darcy held up her glass.

"Drink up," said Brody, "in fact let's all drink to Marco." And they raised their cups, clashing them together and shouted, "TO MARCO!"

Frank started to tear up, "I'm really mad at him for leaving me. Now I'm all alone."

"You still have us," said Darcy.

"I know," and he tried to blow, but actually spit, her a kiss across the table.

"So where's Sara?" asked Brody.

"She phoned me earlier and told me she was off to Africa again," Darcy informed them, "she said it was much safer among the wild animals there than the ones here; or something to that affect."

"I'll drink to that," said Frank and they toasted once more.

"There's something I want to tell all of you before you read it in the paper tomorrow," Brody hesitantly began, "my uncle left everything to me."

"The newspaper?" asked Darcy.

"And his house, his yacht and his fortune."

"Well, looks like you finally made it," said Frank.

"I didn't want it *this* way. And I want to thank you guys for going to his funeral with me. It meant a lot."

"Where else would we be but there supporting our friend?" asked Darcy.

Frank gulped the last of his coffee, "ANOTHER ROUND," he shouted to the absent waitress. He slammed his cup on the table. "Well I got put on temporary suspension with pay and had to submit to a psych evaluation. Now I have to wait until everything's sorted out. What a load of crap," he mumbled, now exhausted. Frank looked around for the waitress, "where's my drink?"

"It's coming," said Darcy, "I'm sorry they're giving you such trouble, Frank, but maybe I can help."

"What can you do that hasn't already been done to me?"

"Not *to* you but *for* you. I've been promoted to lieutenant and temporarily put in charge of your unit."

"You're kidding? They bitch-slap me and pat you on the back? How's that fair?"

"It's not. I believe it's an injustice that perhaps I can take care of before I go on my leave."

"You're leaving me, too?" Frank whimpered.

"Just for a while. I need to get away from work, The City, just everything in general. The Fifth Column left a perplexing and indecent plight in their wake. I need to sort things out for myself."

"Well, while you're doing that, I'm going to be chasing the leads embedded in Duncan's cell phone," Montgomery announced.

"Wow, it's like he's helping you from the grave," said Brody, "weird."

"The really weird part is how much information he was able to pry from his source. I don't know how he managed it, but it puts me miles ahead of where I was."

"So where is Duncan leading you?" Brody inquired.

"I can't tell you or I'd have to kill you," Montgomery jested. And when no one laughed, he said, "Seriously, lighten up you guys, I'm only kidding." Darcy and Frank relaxed and nervously laughed while Brody's eyes instinctively widened.

"That's not funny, especially with what I've been through. *You* may be used to that type of G-man humor but it falls a little close to home for me," chastised Brody.

"Sorry, little man," Montgomery apologized, "perhaps it was in bad taste."

The waitress finally arrived with another round of Irish coffees.

"Keep 'em comin'," a sloshed Frank commanded her.

The group noticed he was not given regular coffee this time, but as they looked at each other, they decided to just let him imbibe.

"I'm going to miss Marco's funeral tomorrow," Montgomery confessed, "and for that, I'm very sorry. He was a true patriot."

"Here, here," said Frank raising his glass for another toast and they all joined him.

Darcy watched Frank spill his drink, "looks like I may have to get Frank ready tomorrow. He's one of the pall bearers."

"Yeah, doesn't appear like he'll be able to pull himself together," Brody concurred, "I'll help you."

"Thanks, Brody, I'll take you up on that."

And with suddenness, Brody was reminded of something he wanted to ask Montgomery.

"Hey, Lulu got away didn't she? Do you know where she went?"

"No, I can't say we've found her yet, or if she was able to make contact with the Fifth Column. But four bodies were found inside the charred wreckage of the house and none of them belonged to her. So we can safely assume that you *did* see her get away."

"I *knew* it," proclaimed Brody, "then do you think we're all safe?"

"Based on my intel I would venture to say we must still remain vigilant."

"That's a little ominous and evasive."

"That's the best I've got."

"Then we'll just have to accept that," Darcy conceded, "we've been dealt worse hands and have come out just fine. I know we will now, too. We have to believe that."

"As long as you remain diligent . . ." began Montgomery.

". . . and prepared," finished Darcy. They both laughed.

"Why's that so funny?" asked Brody, "seems like sound advice to me."

"Well, you see. . . ." Montgomery started.

"Never mind," interrupted Darcy.

"Hey, no private jokes here," Brody protested.

"Here, here," said Frank toasting to himself and downing more of his drink.

"Really, Frank, haven't you had enough yet?" asked Brody.

"I can still see you clearly . . ." Frank muttered as he wobbled unsteadily in his chair, "so, nope."

They all fell silent and into their own private limbo of grief, sadness, misery and relief.

"So why did Sara leave before Marco's funeral?" asked Brody, breaking the silence.

"I asked her the same thing," said Darcy, "she told me she didn't believe in funerals. They were too depressing. She wanted to celebrate Marco's life instead. She said that he'd already left his body. That it was just a shell that carried his spirit."

"Oh, that's too bad," said Montgomery, "I've always felt that funerals were for the living. To come together and comfort one another."

"Either way," Brody gently spoke, "we'll always carry a little piece of Marco with us."

"That's a little like what Sara told me," Darcy concluded, "that he'll always be in her heart."

"Well dead is dead, I say," countered Frank, "Marco's still not coming back."

"Neither is my uncle," Brody reminded him, "but it's going to be up to me to preserve his legacy."

"What legacy?" Frank snapped. "His hands were just as dirty as the rest of 'em."

"I'm speaking of the legacy I remember before we found out what he was doing. He took a struggling rag and turned it into a prosperous and enterprising newspaper. He invested his beliefs in those he hired and kept around him. That's the Bradley Ambrose I want to remember. He made a poor choice in alliances for sure, but I want people to think back on him the way I do."

"That's very decent of you, Brody," said Montgomery, "you do realize though that you've got a monumental undertaking ahead of you?"

"That I do. It's going to take me months to erase the impression the Fifth Column left on the newspaper. But the good thing is that readership has increased immensely. Because of all of you I am privy to details not available to the general public. People want to know, and we're telling them."

"Lemons into lemonade," declared Darcy.

"Then why is it that I'm the only one who's been soured by all this?" asked Frank.

"Because you're letting it," said Darcy, "let me put it this way. You can allow yourself to suffer with grief, pain, anger and disappointment *or* you can take that energy and focus on where you want to be instead."

"Alright then, I want to be alone on the beach on a tropical island."

"Then make it happen."

"That simple?"

"That simple."

"Hey, I think you're on to something here."

Montgomery looked at his watch, "it's getting late and I have an early flight in the morning."

"A flight," sighed Frank, "I can fly on outta here. Anywhere I want to go."

"And I think I need to get Frank home too," Darcy noted.

"Home is where the heart is," Frank bemoaned. He turned to look at the outside TV monitor, and did his best to focus through his double vision. "Hey, isn't that Marco's friend?" He pointed toward the image finding it difficult to steady his arm.

They all turned to look, but there was no sound. Darcy quickly went over and adjusted the volume.

"And in other news we turn to Martin Jackson reporting from the scene where a bomb explosion killed four people, Martin. . . .

Yes, Brian. I'm standing in front of a house on the 2500 block of Fulton Street where it appears several bombs exploded, killing four people, according to the SFPD bomb squad. As you can see behind me the investigation and clean-up is still on-going. We have no reports on the identities of the four bodies and the coroner's report is still pending. Also, just around the corner from here, in front of a row house on the 2700 block of Balboa Street, there was an additional bomb blast that inciner-ated a car and two occupants. This blast occurred just prior to the blast on the house. Unfortunately my close friend and SFPD Detective, Marco Morelli, was a victim in the car blast along with San Francisco Bay Daily reporter, Duncan Brewer.

So to sum it up: police detectives appear to be left with many more questions as to who could be responsible for either or both of these crimes. They are now searching for a person of interest, Lulu Tremblay, for questioning. Back to you, Brian."

"Well, I guess that answers my question," said Brody.

"That bitch," garbled Frank, his speech continuing to deteriorate.

"She's not going to get away with this, is she?" Darcy exclaimed.

"Don't you worry about her," Montgomery attested, "Duncan has given us some very good leads, so to speak. And I'm sure I'll be able to dig her out from whatever rock she's crawled under."

"Do you think she's still here?" asked Brody.

"It's hard to say, but my guess is that she's long gone. Maybe even back in the folds of the Fifth Column somewhere."

"You're going to find her though, aren't you?" Darcy implored. "I don't think I'll ever be able to stop looking over my shoulder until they have her, until I know the Fifth Column is ruined."

"So where are you going to look for her?" Brody was nosing around for more information.

"If I told you that . . . never mind. I'm going overseas, and that's all I can say for now. I've turned over Duncan's phone to my handler at DHS, but not before downloading all the information first. So off to work I go."

"Do you need any help? I mean, I can go with you, you know, just like before." Brody offered.

"No, Brody," Montgomery began, trying his best not to laugh, "not this time."

"Oh really? Then I must have been dreaming all this time because I'm certain we were there to help you this time. And I think you got the best from us!" Darcy retorted.

"You all did your level best to help me solve the mystery of the Fifth Column. Don't get me wrong. For that I will always be grateful. But moving forward, I really need to continue on alone. No offense."

"None taken," Darcy relented.

"I'm still thinking. . . ." impugned Brody.

"I have no idea what you're talking about," Frank slurred.

"Okay, now I really must be getting Frank home." Darcy turned to Montgomery and hugged him. "Good luck, Montgomery." And, to Brody, "it really has been good having you around. See you in the morning," and she gave him a hug and tussled his hair.

Leaving the men, she walked around the table to collect Frank and take him home. She tucked him under her arm and made her way to the sidewalk, she turned and looked back.

"This isn't good-bye, you know. I hate good-byes," said Darcy to Montgomery, "so see you around sometime," she told him, even though she knew it was most unlikely their paths would ever cross again.

Montgomery and Brody continued to watch as she assisted a broken Frank to her car. The two men turned to face each other and shook hands. Mere words could not express what they were thinking and feeling.

"See you around then, Brody, good luck."

"Good luck to you, Montgomery, stay in touch."

∽

At about the same time that Montgomery bid farewell to his colleagues, a lone analyst was seated in a windowless and dreary room; sequestered deep within the NSA's secret tombs. She received an alert from a satellite high above the Pacific Ocean. "Someone's sloppy," she groaned to herself as she clicked open the file. After a hasty evaluation, she tapped a short series of keystrokes and Montgomery's secure phone link vibrated.